Nightmares and Dreams

Lyn Miller LaCoursiere

Published by Kieley Publishing
St. Michael, MN 55376

Photo Adaptation by Melanie Kieley
Edited and cover design by Genny Kieley

ISBN # 978-1-4276-2896-1

2nd printing

A Note from the Author

After it had been buried in the closet for years, I decided it was time to dust off this first manuscript, the beginning of my series. I do this with some hesitation; as a novice I had and still have a lot to learn about writing. Looking back over forty plus years the only thing I had written were grocery lists, checks and an occasional note on a greeting card.

Who had time to be creative? I was a single parent raising four kids, sometimes working three jobs and always tired. Now decades later I realize stretching the menu, clothing the crew, keeping a home and striving to keep the wolf away took one heck of a lot of imagination and certainly qualify as creativity.

I remarried later and had some wonderful years, but after eight months of struggling with an illness my husband died. It was then I joined a grief group and learned the value of journaling. Finally I was on to something! I wrote volumes using yellow legal tablets and Pilot pens. I felt close to God and began writing spiritual poems. Then I saw an ad for "The Center for Developing Writers" at the Hennepin Technical College. I attended that first night on shaky legs, my poems gripped in my sweaty palms. Maureen LaJoy met me at the door and in her sweet voice welcomed me to her class. I looked at her with awe. A real writer! I studied her clothes; her long skirt, belted over-blouse, boots and dangling earrings. So, this was how a writer dresses. I was smitten. I was going to burn my sweat-shirts and jeans and dress glamorously just like her.

That first night I read my work and bless her, she gave me the encouragement I needed. After some time I thought I'd try my hand at contemporary prose, and bravely used the f-word, Maureen gasped at my change of genre, then urged me on with a twinkle in her eye.

Writing opened up a new world for me, and after writing numerous short stories, I used a favorite I'd created with characters Lindy Lewis and Reed Conners and bravely kept on going. Using bits and pieces of my life, people I'd met, places I'd been and of course embellishing, I wrote my first book. I called it Nightmares and Dreams. That was more than ten years ago. In the process of maturing as a writer I'm happy to say it still gets me up and moving most mornings as I am finishing my fourth book about the starcrossed lovers.

Each day of writing is an adventure as my characters make me smile with their antics and cry when their troubles abound.

So here it is, after years in the back of the closet I hope you enjoy my book as Lindy and Reed began their tumultuous journey.

I eagerly look forward to hearing what you, my readers think about this first book. You can e-mail me at lindylewis1@msn.com.

This book is dedicated to the memory of
Maureen LaJoy,
a dear friend and mentor
who encouraged me to keep putting my
thoughts on paper.
Also to my writing buddies
who urged me to start a novel and give
my character Lindy Lewis a home.
Cheers to all of you; especially
Judy, Ross, Janet, Sue, Judd and dear Genny,
who labored diligently over
the "hard stuff" for me.

-1-

Lindy Lewis stood in her old red robe; oddly frozen, watching the flames consume all her possessions and memories. The heat was intense. The flames were as high as the treetops. Sparks flew and exploded in the air, cascading into spiraling tails of color. Clouds of billowing smoke brought stinging tears to the onlookers' eyes as they stood mesmerized at the scene before them.

"Stand back, everyone, please," a burly fireman said in a gruff voice. The early morning March winds carried the smell of hot rubber for blocks and the fireman nervously waved Lindy back, as the paint began to bubble and sizzle on her car parked next to her house. A seed of doubt crept into her mind now, as she watched it all happening.

Maybe, just maybe, she'd made a mistake.

***

There just wasn't enough evidence to continue the search. Tanner Burk had spent months looking for Sierra's killer and had only found one sure detail. It had been a red car that had forced her off the road! It was the one and only clue. The skid marks that led over the edge of the highway and into the ravine anguished him daily.

He sat down at his desk and slid the files over and began to go over them one more time. Somewhere in here is the answer, his instincts told him as he painstakingly read through them again. There were three cases; John Lund, a man he had convicted and sent to prison for book-making. The second one had to do with records Tanner kept on the chief of police. A personal issue he pursued on his own. The last file was from the Reka Holmes case, a multi-millionaire, who had divorced a husband of questionable origins and means. The long nasty trial had resulted in prison time for John Thomas, who was a thief and a con artist.

Burned out and restless, Tanner grabbed the files and locked the office door. He got in his car and headed north to see his friend and former college buddy Reed Conners. Away from the busy turmoil of the big city, into the peaceful rolling hills of cattle country and grain farms

I'm missing something! Maybe together--. He blew out a breath as he drove, alone and in despair.

The familiar ache pierced his heart reminding him again of the love he and Sierra had shared over the years. He put his hand on her file, and felt the coldness of the paper covering the pages of her life.

***

There's millions of dollars out there just waiting for me! His eyes burned deviously as he sat on a bar stool at the Pit, gulping his whiskey and sucking hard on his cigarette. Just out of prison, John Thomas was broke and pissed. His fine clothes, jewelry, cash and easy life with that Holms bitch had gone down the drain with the help of that smart-assed attorney of hers.

Well, maybe not yet! He laughed slyly, then flipped his shoulder length hair off his face, and fingered the phone number in his pocket. Yeah, it helped to have the right friends. For a price his prison pal had promised him a new identity. John Thomas hunched over the bar deep in thought.

Insurance companies, he mumbled and slapped his hand down on the stained wood remembering a conversation with a cell-mate, who was considered one of the slickest swindlers in the pen.

Yeah! I need to get myself a job in one of those goddamn insurance companies and have a front.

He looked around the bar and his eyes fell on Angie, a hard working waitress with a second full time job, and kids that she was raising alone. He needed a place to hang out at while he worked on his plan and she'd be easy.

"Hey Angie, what are you doing after work, wanna get a sandwich?"

Her eyes lit up as she said, "Sure John, I'll be done early!"

-2-

The phone rang with a aggravating shrill one late summer morning breaking into Lindy's dream. She reached out sleepily from under the covers, and fumbled among the books and junk scattered on the bedside table and answered.

"Good morning Miss Lewis," the hotel operator said, "There's a gentleman here to see you. His name is Jud Thurman. Shall I send him up?"

Lindy sat up instantly awake. Jud Thurman, the insurance man! The months of waiting were finally over. This was the day she'd dreamed of, yet dreaded. If things didn't go as she had planned. She swept the hair out of her blue eyes, alert yet cautious.

"Would you ask him to wait ten minutes," she asked. Clunking down the telephone, Lindy jumped out of bed, ran into the bathroom, brushed her teeth, and pulled on a pair of jeans and a sweater. Her red hair hung in flattened strands. She checked herself in the mirror.

God, I really do look pathetic, but it's good. Well girl, this is it, she whispered at her pale reflection. She forced herself to take three slow breaths to calm her shaking nerves and opened the door to a man with short brown hair; gold framed glasses over piercing brown eyes and dressed in a blue pin-striped suit.

"Good morning. Come in, Mr. Thurman." Lindy patted her hair, straightened the shabby clothes she had purposely saved for this. "Excuse my appearance, everything I had was lost in the fire." Her voice held a tremor.

His eyes swept over her quickly. To cover her nervousness, she added, "I'm still trying to forget that horrendous sight of my house and all my things burning."

He cleared his throat, "Miss Lewis I'm sure it's a traumatic time." Jud Thurman unbuttoned his jacket and sat down in one of the two easy chairs in her hotel room. Soberly, he began taking papers out of his briefcase and arranging them in neat piles on the table between them. Early morning traffic hummed just outside. Faint wisps of exhaust crept in through the open window. Her bed was unmade. Magazines, a take-out carton from the restaurant downstairs and empty soda cans were scattered haphazardly around the cramped, faded

Southwestern decorated room. Lindy's heart thundered. She was sure he could hear the thudding crashes banging against her ribs, as she sat perched on the edge of her chair.

She held her breath as he began, "Miss Lewis, after a thorough examination and verification, my company concludes the fire was caused by a short in the wiring which ignited your painting supplies." Lindy exhaled slowly trying to control her nerves.

Jud Thurman placed the papers in front of her and said, "I'll need you to sign these please, and then I'll have the check ready for you!" Lindy grasped the pen he handed her and signed her name on the specified lines, sure she was going to faint from fright and anxiety. He handed her the check then left after wishing her good luck. She closed the door and stared at the check. My God, it was over! She had one million dollars! And, like a kid she hopped up on her bed and began to bounce, up and down, until her hair stood up wildly on her head and her breath ran out.

I'm rich! I'm rich! I'm rich, she sang, and then clapped her hands over her mouth remembering she was in a hotel and the walls were thin. Now finally she could start that new life. Her dream.

Lyn Miller LaCoursiere

-3-

The heavy traffic had thinned out, and Tanner's thoughts went back to Sierra as he drove. He had been in practice for several years when he had decided he needed a secretary to sort out his messy office. A smile crossed his face as he remembered their first meeting.

"Mr. Burke my name is Sierra Ames," she had said confidently. "I've just finished school and this will be my first job using my secretarial skills. I can see you need me!"

Tanner had eyed her with interest, noting the crisp blue suit and matching shoes. Her dark eyes, petite figure and blonde hair-do. He smiled at her confidence and fell in love.

"Well Miss Ames," he recalled saying, "After interviewing numerous people I was just about to give up the search. Then you walked in my door.

You're everything I've been looking for. You've got the job!"

It had seemed that all the cases, the lies and the pathetic characters had all been easier to deal with when she had been there. His life had been centered on his law practice and their being together. They had shared many hours of hard work, coming in early and sometimes not leaving until late in the night. Together they had gradually built a flourishing business and a deep bond had grown between them. Sierra had been gone almost a year now, but he swore he could still smell her perfume in the office, and in his bed. Could it be her spirit still lingering there to comfort him? His eyes were fathomless pools of sadness as he remembered.

As Reed's ranch came into view, Tanner stretched his cramped and tired body; looking forward to a cold beer with his friend. The fading sun sent long shadows over the low-slung roof of the brick ranch-style house. The blinds were closed against the hot afternoon sun promising coolness inside. Reed had given up his office in town years ago, and only took special law cases at his home office. It was surprisingly too quiet.

How long had it been since they'd talked? Right after Sierra's accident, Tanner remembered. He stood for a few minutes on the shaded veranda steps and gazed off into the blue-green hills that he knew Reed loved. Mosquitoes swarmed around his head.

Something was wrong! Reed had a penchant for anything on wheels, and he expected to see his jeep, a pick-up or some range vehicles standing around. But the yard was empty. The last time Tanner had been there, the place had been alive with a flurry of activities; cattle in the pastures, ranch-hands working on fences, and the cook in the kitchen creating wonderful aromas of Spanish dishes. The brown and white Herefords were gone and the grass had grown tall in the pastures.

Where the hell was he?

Tanner walked back to his car, then stood for a minute and looked around at the quiet lonely place. Heavy dew on the prairie grass sent up sweet perfume in the air. The only sounds were the buzzing insects and an occasional hooting owl in the distance. He got into his car and started back down the driveway, his analytic mind working furiously. Suddenly, his foot hit the brake. Gravel burst up in a dusty cloud as he stopped abruptly.

As a criminal lawyer, had Reed run into some kind of trouble? Tanner sat in the silence on the desolate road; his slim body slumped tiredly as he drummed his fingers on the steering wheel. A strand of crisp black hair, tinged with gray fell over his forehead. His blue eyes deep in thought, staring out the open car window, feeling more alone then ever in the middle of nowhere.

***

Tonight's the night! She's got the money! The man ran up the stairs to his apartment and slammed the door. It had taken months but finally she had the settlement. The woman was loaded! At forty-six years old, it had been the hardest work John Thomas, alias Jud Thurman or J.T. for short had ever done. Visions of a new car, clothes and Las Vegas danced across his thoughts. Okay Lindy Lewis, get ready! It was Friday night and J.T.'s plan was ready for phase II.

-4-

L indy had slept a few hours, then she began to toss and turn as the hotel walls were closing in on her after months of waiting. She'd bought a shiny black BMW, and she needed just one good night of sleep before she got on the road to her new life in sunny California.

She punched the pillow in frustration and mumbled. Maybe a drink would help her sleep. She tossed the covers aside, dressed in her designer jeans, her new red silk shirt and high-heeled sandals. She applied her make-up with care and fluffed her hair.

Downstairs, the crowded hotel bar overflowed out into the lobby while the band played the top forty songs. The air filled with smoke and colognes, mixed with charged up expectations as the patrons mingled.

Lindy found a stool at the bar and ordered a brandy Manhattan. As she sipped her drink, her thoughts wandered back to her past. A hundred years ago, it seemed.

Lindy Lewis was now in her early forties. She'd worked hard as a young girl, paying her own way through college, and later, traveled around the country working for a chain of hotels. She leaned into the bar as she held the cocktail to her lips. A lit cigarette smoldered in the ashtray. Lost in thought, her blue eyes saddened at the memory of her husband's death, and the end of that wonderful secure era. Then she remembered the huge ungodly medical bills and the never-ending expensive repairs on their big house.

The brandy burned Lindy's throat and warmed her stomach, but didn't take away the familiar ache as she looked longingly at the couples on the dance floor. She didn't notice a man take the stool next to her. Little did she know he had been waiting for her.

She turned to him as he said, "Hi, I'm new in town. New job. No friends." He reached over and took her hand, "My name's J.T." He was dressed in jeans and a white v-necked sweater. His dark brown hair, curled over his temple. "So what's your name, beautiful?"

Brown eyes gazed into hers. A frown crossed her face for a fleeting moment as something seemed familiar about them. But she pushed that thought out of her mind and thought she'd just been paranoid for too long. She replied, "Lindy."

"Lindy," he said then added, "Would you like to dance?"

She smiled. "It's been a long time J.T. but I'd love to."

The sensuous look he gave her as he stood up sent shivers of heat though her body. A feeling she had forgotten. The band swung into a slow love song as he took her hand and led her onto the dance floor. The beat of the drums echoed in her ears as they swayed to the music. When the number ended, she felt his arm around her waist, the slight pressure of his hip against hers as they walked back to their seats. As Lindy settled on her stool, he bent over and kissed her, then traced a finger over her face, circling her lips. Enthralled, Lindy leaned closer and inhaled his cologne.

J.T. raised his glass. "Here's to us, Lindy, we were made for each other." They danced again, each time their bodies strained closer.

"Why don't you come up to my room for a night cap?" J.T. asked at the end of the evening. Having drunk more than she normally would, Lindy threw caution to the wind, and agreed. They walked to his room holding hands.

Soft music played on the radio, as they sat on the davenport and J.T. talked about being transferred to Minneapolis from New York and his job at IBM. Lindy was absolutely taken by his charm but for a moment again, she wondered why his eyes seemed somewhat familiar? She promptly forgot the uneasy thought, as he put his glass down on the table and took her in his arms.

"Lindy," he whispered as his lips captured hers again, "I need you!"

Just this once, she thought as J.T. began kissing her neck, her throat. It had been so long since anyone needed her. Minutes later, he did things with his tongue to her nipples that sent rapturous pangs of joy to her senses. He undressed her, and covered her stomach with more fluttering kisses. Time stood still for Lindy as a new world opened and J.T. began making love that was so intense, so erotic, and so extremely personal she was beyond protesting. Her body pulsated with rocking emotions, as her world exploded into a million fragments sending an ecstasy of tremors though her body.

-5-

Tanner drove aimlessly, his mind in a shambles. What the hell had happened, Reed had disappeared!

They'd talked about getting together and going fishing in Wisconsin when he had called Reed again about Sierra's accident, but that had been almost a year ago. Now it was the middle of the summer, the pastures were empty and the grass ankle deep. Not a sign of life anywhere.

The small town they had both grown up in lay ahead as he anxiously barreled down the highway hours later. He checked in at the Dew Drop Inn, tossed his bags on the bed and went down the one and only street to the Rex cafe.

Home Cooked Meals served daily, a blackboard sign proclaimed. Tanner stood for a moment in the entry and gazed around. The front of the cafe had been redecorated. Shelves had been brought in to display crafts created by the locals. Crocheted afghans, quilts, flower arrangements and small trinkets tumbled from tables. As he stepped in further, the aroma of roast pork and spiced apples set his stomach to growling. He remembered the same tables were once covered in red and white-checkered oilcloths. Lacy curtains graced the windows. The small cozy cafe hummed with activity on this Friday night as the local patrons visited with neighbors and listened to Lawrence Welk on a huge television mounted over the counter. Tanner tiptoed up behind a familiar figure and whirled the woman around in a waltz.

"Hello Aunt Julia," he whispered in her ear. The lady's aged face crinkled up in a smile as she fell into step with one of her favorite nephews.

"Tanner Burke, you rascal. It's about time you came and visited me!" She smoothed her permed hair and adjusted the homemade apron that covered her cotton dress.

"I know it's been a few years. Business is looking good." Tanner took a seat at the counter.

"Young man you look like you could use a good meal." His Aunt busied herself setting out silverware and a paper napkin as she studied his thin frame. "Honest to goodness, are you purposely starving yourself?"

Tanner smiled at this woman who had been like a mother to him after his parents had died suddenly when he was a young boy. He drained the glass of water she set before him and grinned, "Nah, just busy, I guess."

"Well, Arnie will fix a plate for you right away." She hurried to collect from a family that stood at the cash register waiting to pay their bill, murmuring something about those awful big cities.

Tanner slept fitfully on the hard mattress in his motel room that night, finally, at the first hint of dawn gave up all thoughts of resting and went outside, hoping to catch an early morning breeze. It was hot and still.

-6-

It feels so wonderful to be loved, Lindy murmured as she sprayed herself with perfume. Infatuated with J.T.'s intense courting she stayed in town longer than she expected and still lived in the hotel. Her thoughts were on the special night she had planned; strawberries and champagne and a new CD. She smiled at herself in the floor length mirror and was satisfied that the vibrant green dress swirled effectively just above her knees. Sheer black nylons and patent pumps accentuated her shapely legs. Running down the steps, she hopped in her new car and raced out of the parking ramp.

On the ten-minute drive to J.T.'s new apartment in the nearby suburb, Lindy's voice rambled over songs they had danced to in the few weeks they had been dating. She sped along in anticipation and parked next to his car in the parking lot. When she reached to get her bag of groceries out of the back of her BMW, scattered papers lying on the ground next to his vehicle caught her eye. Curiously, she put the groceries down and gathered them up, then dumb-founded, picked up a blonde wig and a pair of glasses. As she began to read the papers, she gaped at a page containing detailed reports of her every move. Check stubs from the Federated Insurance Company made out to someone named Jud Thurman, incidentally, which was her insurance company. Identification and a social security card made out in this name. She stood frozen as a chill swept up her back, the warmth of her silk dress turned to ice as she realized something ominous was going on.

My God, those brown eyes, that's why there had been something familiar about the two men! And as if burned, she dropped the wig, glasses and the papers to the ground. Then left the champagne and strawberries on the curb and ran to her car.

J.T. was Jud Thurman!

-7-

A gut feeling had been shadowing Tanner all night again, and edges of danger crawled up and down his spine as he stood on the corner of Broadway and 8th in the early dawn.

"What the hell is it?" he mumbled under his breath. A whiff of fried bacon from his Aunt Julia's café mingled with the fumes of the dry cleaners up the block as the small town businesses began to prepare for opening at sunrise.

***

In Minneapolis, J.T. clenched the phone to his ear. His brown eyes fierce after going out to his car and discovering the bag of groceries Lindy had promised to bring over for their special night earlier, sitting on the ground. The incriminating papers and disguise he used to fool her were there too. He must have dropped them when he got out of the car.

"The bitch probably figured it out," he roared as he punched a wall. Angry sweat broke out on his face. "Pick me up," he bellowed to his buddy. A few minutes later, he jumped into Jones's red car and sped off.

***

Lindy sat on the bed in her hotel room stunned after finding the papers and disguise. As painful tears coursed down her face, she remembered that niggling feeling of doubt that had plagued her all along about not leaving town immediately after getting the insurance money.

Why hadn't she paid attention to her instincts and not gotten involved with J.T.? All of a sudden a terrifying thought pierced through her remorse as her mind raced.

He didn't want her, he wanted her money!

She caught her breath and stood up on trembling legs. As soon as he discovers his papers, the wig and the glasses on the ground, he'll know I was there. Then when he finds the bag of champagne and strawberries I left on the curb, he'll know for sure I was there. The evidence was incriminating.

Her heart jammed wildly in her chest as she tossed her clothes in a suitcase, ran down the hotel stairway to the underground parking area and stepped into her black BMW.

***

Minutes earlier, J.T. got in Jones's red car and said, "Go by that broad's hotel and then out to the airport!"

"What the hell are you going there for; she's probably got the cops waiting for you?" Jones's deep voice vibrated.

"Fuck, I just need five minutes to settle a score with that bitch before I split this goddamn town!" He inhaled hard on his cigarette. Just as they came off the parkway and turned into the hotel entrance, Lindy's car shot past them.

"There she is, in that black BMW. Follow the bitch," J.T. yelled as the red Lincoln flew into the Saturday night traffic as if it had wings.

-8-

Lindy put the powerful BMW in drive and raced down the dark hotel ramp. Her breath froze in her throat as she saw the familiar face of J.T. outlined by a streetlight, sitting in the passenger seat of a red car.

Dear God, help me, she whispered as she flew out to the freeway. With her eyes glued to the road and her hands in a viselike grip on the wheel, she prayed he hadn't seen her. However, a short distance behind her J.T. yelled, "That was her! Okay pal, let's see what this pussy car of yours can do!"

Traffic was heavy even though it was late at night and everyone was going north to get an early start on the long weekend. A steady stream of cars, bikers, vans, pickups with campers all traveling at break-neck speed as the urgency to get away snaked its way along the pavement, and covered the faces of the drivers and passengers.

Jones gunned the motor, recklessly weaved in and out amongst the traffic, and caught up with Lindy. He tapped her bumper with his. Her car swerved, coming dangerously close to a deep embankment as she fought for control.

"Hit her again, push her over!" J.T. yelled, then twisted around and checked the back window as the air suddenly reverberated with an ear-deafening roar. He gaped at the scene unfolding behind their red car. His voice cracked as he said, "Fuck, you won't believe this man; the whole fucking town is behind us on their Harleys." J.T. watched bug-eyed, as they were surrounded by black leather and exhaust fumes, closing them in. A sea of black helmets and goggles; an army of faceless monsters on thundering bikes were slowing them down.

"Goddamn, she's getting ahead!" They watched as the taillights on the powerful black car sailed out of sight in the late night traffic.

"Fuck, we lost her! Pull off on the next exit," J.T. yelled and slammed his fist into the dash.

***

Tanner Burke stood outside the motel, one shiny boot propped up on a rock lying by the sidewalk. Beads of sweat glistened on his forehead.

Now in his middle forties, Tanner had learned to trust his instincts. He warily scanned the quiet streets of his home town. He took one last drag of his cigarette, impatiently flipped the butt into the street and watched it hit the ground sending sparks flying. Just then a shiny black BMW roared up to the stop sign. A woman sat at the wheel, hunched over and clutching it for dear life. Tanner stood just a few feet from her car as she hesitated at the sign. He recognized Lindy Lewis, his pal Reed Conner's girl-friend from college days, and he saw that raw fear shadowed her face as if she was racing for her life. As she flew on by, he wondered, could Sierra have been chased by someone too?

**

A block away, J.T. slumped down in Jones's red car, his body tense. He had been outsmarted by Lindy and the bikers. The Lincoln slowed down as it approached a stop sign in the small town. As they neared the street corner, his breath hissed and he bolted upright in the seat and yelled, "Jesus, that man standing there is Tanner Burke, my ex-old lady's attorney!" Spittle flew in the air. "Son of a bitch, he sent me to jail!" J.T. reached for his gun and aimed. "By God, I'll make him dance now!"

In that instant, J.T. and Tanner Burke's eyes met in recognition.

As the ear-splitting shot rang out, Tanner hit the ground. Jesus Christ! He'd been right all along. The wait was over. Another shot blasted through the air, closer this time, and the smell of gunpowder and dust hung in the air.

There it was--, a split second disclosure! John Thomas was in the car. The man he had sent to jail. It all fit. John Thomas was Sierra's killer!

More shots peppered the air and time stood still as Tanner lay there hugging the earth, the pavement. The sudden stillness brought a crackling reality. He was going to die! J.T.'s gun pointed directly at him, and another bullet cut though the air with a scream. It was too late...too late to run. There wasn't any time. Time had run out. The air vibrated as the weight of death hung suspended.

With a deafening burst of force, his world shattered into a blur of nothingness as his life flowed across the cement in rivers of red. Tanner Burke lay dead in a pile of twisted humanity as a train whistle, miles away, sent out lonely calls of departure.

Adrenalin pumped though J.T.'s veins as he and Jones flew though the rest of the small town. He laughed, turned to Jones and said, "Fuck man that felt great. Let's stop at the casino up ahead, my luck has just changed!"

-9-

Lindy ran into the brightly lit casino. Her insides trembled after more than two hours on the highway being chased by J.T. Thank God for those bikers who had apparently seen what was happening and jumped to her defense. She found a restroom, put her purse down on the sink and looked at her haggard face in the mirror, then whimpered in desperation.

How had she gotten into this?

She washed the mascara from her tear stained face as she worried. Had J.T. still been somewhere close behind her on the freeway and did he see her turn into the entrance to the casino? If he had followed her, could she hide among the throngs of people and escape through a side door?

The Great Casino was jammed as Lindy stepped out of the restroom and cautiously made her way though the aisles of slot machines and black jack tables. Bells shrilled as bleary-eyed patrons joyfully collected their winnings from the machines.

As Lindy searched for J.T. among the crowds of people milling around; her heart jumped in her chest when a man called her name. She counted the steps to the nearest exit, and then quickly searched the faces of the people sitting at the nearby gaming tables. Her frightened glance fell on a man she had known years ago. He had been in law school then while she was studying for her degree in business. They'd had a torrid love affair and lived together for several years.

Her heart began to spin as she recognized Reed Conners.

***

"Are you still drinking those rum drinks?" Reed teased as they sat in the lounge a few minutes later.

Lindy clasped her hands under the table, willing herself to relax. She tried to smile.

Older now, Reed's reddish hair had turned to a sandy color and was mixed with gray. Lines were scattered around his blue eyes. Clad in a brown sport coat, a soft yellow shirt opened low to a broad chest.

"Lindy, it's been years!   Where have you been?" he continued.

She replied hesitantly, "Well, I live in Minneapolis now. I got married and quit my job." Sadness crossed her face as she went on, "And, it's been almost a year now since my husband died."

Reed reached for her hand. Her mind raced as she wondered, did he still care? Would he help her?

"What about you Reed, are you still living on your ranch?" she asked.

Reed sat back and threw an arm over the top of the booth. "Nope, I pulled up stakes and sold out."

"You did! What about your law practice?"

"I gave most of that up." Reed laughed, "Midlife crisis I guess, I needed a change. Things were starting to get to me. But I still work part time as an insurance investigator." Lindy's breath caught. Oh God, did he know about her house fire? No, not likely. It would be too much of a coincidence; there were hundreds of insurance companies.

Her eyes brightened as an idea occurred to her, and she asked innocently, "Do you still have your cabin at the lake?"

Reed smiled again, "Yup, I sure do, and that's where I live now."

Just then Lindy glanced at a mirror that reflected the entrance into the lounge and to her horror saw J.T. walk by. He was here, at the casino! She willed her nerves to be still as she asked, "Just for old times sake, would you consider letting me stay for a day or two at your place Reed? I was on my way up north to visit relatives and had to stop here when I suddenly got a migraine!" She ran a hand over her forehead.

"Well sure Lindy," Reed said, "You know the way--the key is under the red flower pot on the deck."

She leaned over and squeezed his hand.

"Hey Lindy," he added, "I'm working on something now so I'll probably be hung up for a day or two, but wait for me!"

"Okay. Thanks Reed," Lindy replied. "We've got a lot to catch up on." She glanced around the lounge quickly and stood up to leave. With a quick smile of thanks she slid out a side door.

Within thirty minutes she was at Reed's cabin. She should be safe there until she dared go back to Minneapolis to get her money and leave town again for good!

Moonlight sparkled on the quiet lake, frogs croaked in the distance and a gentle breeze whispered through the birch trees as Lindy looked for the red flowerpot on Reed's deck. The cabin had totally changed from the time she'd last stayed there with him years ago, not only on the outside, but the inside as well.

Lindy looked at the tastefully remodeled rooms with awe. Reed had changed it from an old log cabin to an elegant rustic home. Floor to ceiling windows faced the water, wood floors with wooly rugs scattered here and there, and oversized burgundy leather furniture sat in front of a stone fireplace with overflowing bookcases lining the sides.

Exhausted, she rummaged in a dresser and found a pair of flannel pajamas and crawled into his bed. Tonight she felt safely hidden from J.T., but what about tomorrow?

Several days passed and Reed had not come back. Lindy waited for him, but she had already stayed longer than she'd planned. As much as she hated to, she had to leave in the morning. Money in Minneapolis and sunny California beckoned her.

It was a warm fall day as she sat out on the dock enjoying the scenery. Suddenly, footsteps echoed on the boards. She looked up with a start, and then froze as she saw two men coming towards her. Horrified, she recognized J.T. accompanied by a black man. She scrambled to her feet, ready to run for her life and then realized they had her trapped on the long dock. It stretched forty feet out over deep swirling water and she couldn't swim!

"Bitch, you can't get away now can you?" J.T. raged. As he came toward her, he slid his belt off.

Lindy stared in horror as it snaked though the air making a cutting sound. She shifted her glance for a second to the black man and saw he held a gun. It was pointed straight at her. A scream began deep in her throat, as a shot rang out freezing the moment into a frame of stillness. No one moved. The belt in J.T.'s hand stopped in mid-air. The gunman swung around frantically looking for the new target.

Just then Reed Conner's voice cut through the silence as he shouted, "Okay assholes, don't even breath!" Gravel flew through the air as police cars screeched to a stop in Reed's driveway.

***

"There's more to this story isn't there," Lindy said as she rolled up the sleeves of the shirt she'd borrowed from Reed's closet. Her face was pale. They were sitting at the table in his kitchen later that day after everything had settled down and J.T. was on his way to jail. It had been four days since she'd left the hotel in Minneapolis. A breeze billowed the curtains out over the windowsills and fresh coffee bubbled in the pot on the stove.

"Lindy, you didn't know what you were getting yourself into when you got tangled up with that man," Reed said shaking his head. "I recognized the man you knew as J.T. at the casino too. I've been following him the last few days. That's why I'm late getting here now.

She gaped at him. "You know him?"

"Yes, I've been working on this for some time now!" Reed got up and poured two cups of coffee and settled in again at the table. "Lindy let me start at the beginning. You remember Tanner Burke, my best friend? He put a man named John Thomas in prison for a bank robbery. Then he represented Thomas's wife, Reka Holmes when she divorced him. Sometime later, Tanner's secretary Sierra Ames was killed in a mysterious car accident. We got together several times, but all we had was that it involved a red car. The case was never solved, but Tanner would not let it go. You may as well know Lindy; I work for the same insurance company that insured you. Sometime after your claim was paid out, new evidence was unexpectedly found and I was put on the case to investigate.

"You knew about my fire?" Lindy's eyes were wide as she waited for his reply.

"Yes Lindy." Reed shifted his glance from her stare.

Lindy raised her voice, "Well, why didn't you tell me you knew about my fire when we were at the casino?"

"I'm sorry Lindy, but it wasn't the right time. I have to ask, did you set the fire? Be honest now!"

Maybe it was too late and she was caught, but she still protested, "It was an accident!"

"Lindy, my company wants the million dollars back. I'm sorry to have to be the one to break the news, but I just found out you've been charged with fraud!"

Lindy sat stunned and stared in unbelief. Not now, after all she'd been through! Seconds went by and she realized Reed was still talking, "Lindy, listen to this. I'd been keeping an eye on a new guy my company hired, by the name of Jud Thurman. Now, we know he is John Thomas and the same man who called himself J.T. He killed Sierra Ames, Tanner's girlfriend, and now Tanner!"

Lindy sat frozen, but forced herself to recover. She'd been haunted by J.T.'s brown eyes. The man who had delivered the check for a million dollars from Reed's insurance company to her at the hotel.

She sat in shocked silence, and then repeated weakly, "J.T. killed Tanner?"

Pain deepened the lines in Reed's face. "Yes, I haven't had time yet--." Reed was silent and lost in thought. He looked back at Lindy.

Aghast, Lindy's face became whiter. "My God, I've been involved with a murderer?"

"Afraid so Lindy, but he'll get prison for life!"

Lindy sat clutching the coffee cup in her shaking hands. Then she began to sob. Reed stood up and put a hand on her shoulder, then pulled her into his arms. What started as a comforting embrace soon developed into a kiss, bringing to the surface all the same feelings they had shared years ago. She clung to him, feeling the safety in his arms.

The next morning Reed said, "Lindy, you've got to return the money."

"I will," she promised solemnly as they sat in Reed's living room on the burgundy leather couch drinking coffee after a night of lovemaking and enjoying the warmth of the fireplace. The skies were gray with the feel of an early frost in the air.

"Lindy," Reed ran a hand over her bare leg, "After we get things straightened out with the police and my company, we've got to talk."

Lindy shivered at his touch. She'd thought of nothing else during the wakeful hours in the night and had made up her mind.

She smiled.

He leaned over and took her in his arms, then said, "Lindy, I've got to go to the memorial service for Tanner this morning, but I'll be back shortly. Be ready and we'll take off for Minneapolis."

The sun cast a rosy glow over the still lake. A call from a loon echoed in the stillness as Lindy walked him out to his car. She leaned in through the car window and kissed him, then stepped back.

"I'll see you in a couple of hours," he said.

Lindy smiled and waved. But a few minutes later, the peace in the north was shattered as a black BMW roared off onto the highway.

-10-

Lindy Lewis made one quick stop in Minneapolis and now, days later had finally reached her destination. Her mouth had watered for a good meal the last few miles when the signs along the way had said, "Visit Tony's Steakhouse for a Taste of Splendor!" Now finally, she was there. She got out of her car and leisurely stretched. Just then, a gloved hand grabbed her, covered her mouth, and shoved her stumbling away from the car. Within seconds, a man was behind the wheel of her black BMW speeding away as Lindy lay in the parking lot of Tony's Restaurant in Dallas, Texas.

A scream started in her throat and her lips formed the word, "help!" Then stopped. She couldn't call the police! By now, there probably was a nation wide alert out for her arrest. Nausea swept up her throat as she slumped to the hard packed dirt. She gasped for air. Stunned, in the shadow of a tree with her head in her hands, Lindy huddled, hopeless and alone. All her planning had been for nothing!   She had hesitated, when Reed had come back into her life, but after the long months of waiting for her insurance money to come through, she couldn't give it back. She finally had what she wanted. Now in seconds, her fortune and her beautiful black BMW was gone.

Maybe the thief would come back, she thought hopefully as she wiped her eyes. Sure, she grimaced, won't he be surprised when he found her money. Anger shot through her at the thought of someone else having her money and her car. Exhausted from the trip from northern Minnesota, nervously watching the road behind her, and now, this.

It was 8:30, Saturday night in Dallas. The skies were velvety black and stars so bright; they looked as if you could reach up and touch them. The warm, humid, autumn air laced with the exhaust from charcoal-broiled steaks. Lindy brushed herself off and on shaky legs walked over to the restaurant.

"The Biggest Bar in Texas," it proclaimed on the door. Everything claimed that here. Her shoulders slumped and her stomach ached, both from hunger and fear as she stood uncertainly.

Could she call Reed for help? If she told him what had happened, would he come and help her?

What was she thinking? There was a warrant out for her arrest! Oh God, she panicked, if the police found her, would they believe the money had been stolen from her?

She straightened her sweater and long denim skirt. Then she wiped dust off her high heeled sandals and felt to make sure her ruby and diamond earrings were still safely clipped on her ears.

"They always bring me good luck," she remembered her mom saying years ago. Now they were the only things left of any value to her.

Lindy squared her shoulders, walked in and found a stool at the horse-shoe shaped bar. Mirrors magnified the crowded room that opened into the dining area where huge framed pictures of country singers graced the walls, along with white linen covered tables set with wine glasses. Linda Ronstadt's voice whispered about lost loves over the sound system.

"Hi, what'll you have?" the bartender asked. His wide grin showed perfect white teeth. His blonde hair curled down on his forehead framing his tanned face. The air in the large rooms, cool and heavenly dry as Lindy Lewis sat at the bar in Dallas, without a cent in her pocket. She didn't even have a purse.

"I'll have a brandy Manhattan please," she said boldly but needed both hands to lift the glass to her mouth. The bracing sting of the brandy burned in her throat as unbelief still burned her thoughts.

Where would she go and what would she use for money now? She would need clothes and food.

The audacity of the man who had so silently and expertly stolen everything she owned. She took another sip of her drink and felt the warmth giving her strength. "By God," she vowed, "I'll find him!"

But, why did I take all the money out of the bank when I left Minneapolis? She argued silently with herself. And in cash! Well, what else could I do? I couldn't leave it there. J.T. was after it and then Reed wanted it back! Her facial expression flickered. With a stab of guilt, she remembered their love-making just a few days ago. His advice to turn herself in and return the money. And the look in his eyes as he drove away from his cabin up north that morning.

Could it have meant he thought there might be a future together for them after all? If so, it just wouldn't have been enough. She had fought too hard for her fortune!

She took a sip of the brandy. Well, maybe it was dishonest to burn your own house down for the insurance money. But she needed it to find happiness again; away from all the memories in that old place. She blew out her breath. Well, here she was thousands of miles away and her plan had exploded in her face! She sat deep in misery, unaware of the eyes of a Texan that were on her.

"Would you like to dance?" A southern drawl interrupted her thoughts.

Lindy snapped, "No!" She didn't have time for this.

"Whoa little lady, pardon me!" The man stepped back at her explosive remark, but another drink appeared in front of her.

The restaurant hummed with business as Lindy looked around. After sipping on her second drink, she'd made up her mind. She didn't have a choice. She'd call Reed Conners and turn herself in. It would mean jail, she was sure, but maybe he'd still help her. Hadn't he loved her once?

Could she describe the man who had assaulted her and stolen the car? Reed would ask. Although it had happened in seconds, Lindy remembered he'd worn a red bandanna over his hair, dark glasses, and had a swarthy complexion. He'd come out of nowhere and pushed her out of the way with such force she'd doubled over trying to get her breath before she hit the ground.

The liquor swirled around in her brain, giving her new insights. Her mind worked furiously. If she could figure out a way to stay here for awhile, maybe she'd find the asshole herself. She had a plan.

"Could I see the manager please," she asked the bartender. He eyed her with interest as he picked up the phone. As Lindy waited she smoothed her denim outfit, fluffed her tousled brunette hair. Minutes later a man with a limp came over, his face harried.

"I'm Archie the manager, can I help you?"

"I'm new in town and looking for a job," Lindy said as steadily as her voice could manage. His eyes slid over her face and body with apparent approval. He asked her name.

"Well Lindy, do you know any thing about the restaurant business?" His eyes darted anxiously back to a crowd of people standing impatiently at the dining room door. He ran his hand over his forehead and muttered, oh shit!

"Yes, I do, I was with the Royal chain for fifteen years."

"You were? Well, come with me, Miss Lindy Lewis."

"You mean right now?" Lindy looked at him in surprise.

"Yes, if you know how to take care of this mess, the job is yours. The other hostess walked off the floor and quit tonight." Lindy slid off the bar stool, her head in a whirl after the two Manhattans she'd drank.

"We'll talk later; just see what you can do about these people!" He walked away throwing his hands in the air.

What the hell am I doing? I was just going to stop and eat and then go to a chic hotel. Now look at me! Penniless, hungry, and asking for a job. Frustration deepened the lines on her face. Inside of seconds, she'd gone from rich and independent to a pauper. For a moment, she wandered back in time to when she'd been a happy housewife and content.

A short time later, Lindy had things under control in the dining room. A comfortable hum lulled the busy place as Tammy Wynnet's husky voice told the ladies to "Stand by their Man." Western hats and boots mingled with designer clothes and diamonds. Finally to Lindy's relief, closing time loomed ahead. Her sandaled feet ached, her back felt broken and her head throbbed with a crashing pain. She fell into a chair.

"Hey Lindy, you handled that like a breeze!" Archie sat down with her at a table.

"Thanks," she said and grimaced as she slid a blistered foot out of her shoe.

"Do you want the job?" he asked anxiously.

Lord, she didn't want to go back to that grind but answered, "Yes, I'll take the job, when can I start?"

"You've already started. It's five nights a week and pays five hundred dollars every Saturday. You new in town Lindy?" He looked her over again.

"Yes, I just flew in from Chicago. My luggage was lost, and with it my traveler's checks." The words even amazed Lindy as they flew out of her mouth so easily.

"There's a motel just next door where you can stay. I can advance you some money, if you need it," Archie said.

What choice did she have?

It took all her energy to walk next door to the motel. L. Lewis, she printed on the register at the front desk.

"Do you want some help with your luggage," the sleepy man at the desk asked.

"Not tonight thanks, I'll get it later." Lindy grabbed the key and turned to find her room.

The Lucky Eight was like thousands of other transient motels in the world. One room with a worn beige carpet. A sagging bed, covered with a plaid brown and orange spread with matching drapes. Pictures of cactus and sunsets adorned the room. A bathroom crammed into a closet sized room. The air cool, but held a reminder of thousands of bare feet, that had been in and out of the place. Lindy looked around with disgust, but dead on her feet, tossed her clothes on a chair and slipped between the sheets. Tonight, she needed to sleep. Her last thought was maybe she'd wake up tomorrow and all this would have been just a bad dream!

***

"Twenty-five dollars!" the greasy haired pawn-broker said "Take it or leave it."

"But they're worth more than that. They were my Mother's!" Lindy stepped back as his foul breath assailed her nose.

"Not to me, I've got tons of this junk." His hands pointed to the rows of jewelry arranged in the glass counter. Lindy was inside Al's in the seedy part of Dallas.

How dare he handle her precious earrings like they were junk!

"Is that all I can get?" She asked as she reached over to snatch them back.

The man's attitude was indifferent as he stood with hands in his pockets and said, "Lady, I'm doing my best."

Resigned, Lindy shook her head sadly. "Okay, but promise you won't sell them. I'll be back."

"You got thirty days."

Lindy clasped the money in her hand and left, feeling really empty now without her precious earrings. The money Archie had loaned her paid her room for the week. Now she had twenty five dollars for clothes and make-up. She'd have to go without food until she got to work each day. She stood on a street corner and looked around. Boarded up store-fronts and strip bars stood forlornly in the harsh sunshine. Music throbbed through the morning dampness from Josie's. The smell of stale whiskey and cigarette smoke spiraled out from two doors down. She hailed a passing taxi and hurried into the back seat.

"Is there a thrift shop around here?" Lindy asked the driver.

The Spanish man looked at her in the rear-view mirror. "You're in luck lady, right around the corner."

A combination of moth-balls and potpourri sickened Lindy as she walked into the shop. She needed clothes, shoes and a purse. The sliding tin hangers rasped over the metal bars as she went through the used clothing. She bargained for the price and left. The same taxi driver came around the block and stopped for her.

After getting back to her motel, Lindy threw her purchases on an easy chair, and lay back down in her crumpled bed. She raised her hand to her head and massaged her aching temple. It had been months since the house fire, then the worry and finally the exhilaration when she received the check from the insurance company. Now it seemed like years ago. A shattering sob shook her body and echoed in the motel room.

At four-thirty, Lindy walked back across the steaming hot parking lot wearing her second-hand clothes and into Tony's. She punched the time-clock.

-11-

The days and nights flew by for Lindy. She hadn't worked so hard in years. When her shift ended at midnight, she'd limp back to her room next door at the motel and fall into an exhausted sleep. She'd bought new clothes and gradually settled into a routine. But her insides burned with fury over the situation she was in. At work, she tried to keep a smile on her face, but alone in her room she paced the floor. That morning, she awakened with a plan. Rummaging through the drawers of the dresser for a phone book, she looked up the number of a private investigator and scheduled an appointment.

It had been a hectic week with a convention in town and hundreds of people eager for food and drink. At the end of another hard night at Tony's restaurant in Dallas, she leaned back against the backrest of a stool at the bar and tried to relax after the last customer had been satisfied. Several minutes later, a voice interrupted her exhausted thoughts.

"I stopped in again to see if you would dance with me!"

Lindy looked up into piercing blue eyes and recognized the same man that had approached her on the first night she'd come into the restaurant. That fatal night! The same white hat was pulled down rakishly over one eye. Lonely and flattered by this man's persistence, she looked him over with interest. He had a Clint Eastwood look about him. Slim and muscled. Deep lines edged in a weathered face. A Rolex watch on his wrist and wearing perfectly fitted jeans. His cologne; aggressive and musky, added to the mystery.

"This time I will," Lindy said, forgetting about her aching feet and tired back.

He took her arm and led her onto the dance floor. For a few minutes they danced in silence as their bodies touched lightly. Then relaxing into each other's embrace, he pushed his hat back on his head and pulled her closer. The beat of the music, slow and sensual.

"I'm surprised to see you here." Dade looked down at her and went on, "I just got back into town and decided to stop in."

Lindy smiled. "I work here now."

He stepped back without missing a beat. "Really?"

Lindy replied casually, "Just a job to do until something better comes along." Dade began to hum along to the song as he held her fast in his arms. When the number ended he asked, "Do you mind if I join you?"

Feeling somewhat interested now, Lindy replied, "No, but I don't even know your name."

"It's Dade Lampart." He put his hand out, "What's yours beautiful?"

Hesitating just a bit, she told him. "Lindy Lewis."

Dade tipped his hat. "Well, it's my lucky day. Can I buy you a drink? A Manhattan?"

Lindy had to admit it felt good to have the attention of this man and smiled into his eyes. "I'd love one," she replied. The bartender placed her drink in front of her and winked at Dade. "I see you've met our Lindy here, Mr. Lampart."

"Yes," Dade answered and put an arm over her shoulder. "I wonder where she's been all my life."

Lindy inhaled his cologne and felt his thigh pressed against her leg. God, I'm always taken by a man like this, she cautioned herself; muscled and wearing an expensive scent.

"Where did you come from Lindy?" Dade raised his whiskey to his lips.

Should she tell him, she pondered. Maybe not. "I'm from Chicago," she said as she smiled into his blue eyes.

"Chicago, a crazy place!" He raised his glass again. "I've been there numerous times but that was ages ago. Now you couldn't drag me back!"

"It's a different world here," Lindy said running her hand through her hair. "Everything is big and grand, including egos."

He pulled his hat lower and grinned, "You're right, I'm still trying to find out why that is!"

Lindy sipped her Manhattan. She felt his eyes go over her.

"Jamie Lee Curtis," he said suddenly standing back.

"What---?"

"That's who you remind me of. Yup, that's who!" He crooked his head and looked at her sideways.

"Is this a compliment?" Lindy asked curiously.

"Of course," he lifted her chin and smiled into her eyes. They danced again.

Dade's arm went over her shoulder as he asked, "How about another Manhattan?"

Now she noticed his broad chest as she turned to face him. Wanting to reach in his shirt and run her hands over it, she realized the drink had gone to her head. Wary now, Lindy slid off the bar stool and steadied herself. Another drink would be dangerous.

She tried to hide a hiccup as she smiled and left reminding herself, she didn't have time for a romance, she had to find her car and her fortune!

The next day she met Pug Harris, the detective.

-12-

The phone rang with a consistent complaint cutting into the peace of the north country.

"Conners," the caller barked, "Find that woman and get my million dollars back!" Before Reed could reply to his boss Ed's irate statement the line went dead. He put the receiver down with a bang.

What the hell! So far he'd found the man that had invaded their company--the same man who killed his friend, Tanner Burke and Tanner's girlfriend Sierra Ames. The police were happy about that. But, Lindy Lewis still had the million dollars.

Was he purposely dragging his feet?

At first he'd waited for a phone call from Lindy. Not wanting to believe she'd used him, he'd been optimistic. But as the first days went by, the grim truth sank in. She'd disappeared with the million dollars without a trace. He'd been angry and sad. Christ, he could have helped her out of this trouble, if she'd given the money back. He reported her missing and began to check for credit card charges.

But what a fool he'd been! His thoughts went back to their relationship. It was back in the late seventies when they'd met while they were both attending the University of Minnesota. He'd been studying for a law degree, and she, business finance. He'd worked as a cook in a hamburger joint and when she'd come in looking for a job as a waitress. The first time their eyes met, sparks ignited their young bodies. He remembered the back booth in the dingy cafe where they sat and studied between customers. The awful diet of greasy food they consumed because it was free. Their special nights out when they pooled their precious money and ate somewhere else.

Reed Conners sat at his desk, his chin resting on his raised hand as he stared off into space. Lines etched his fair skin. His shoulders had broadened and a slight paunch had appeared these last years. He got up from his desk and walked into the kitchen and poured another cup of coffee. It seemed like yesterday that she'd sat right there in his shirt and sipped her coffee. Irritated at himself for his thoughts, he went back to his desk in his office and stared out the window at the smooth lake. A call from a loon echoed across the water as the bird looked for his mate. Spirals of fog hung off in the distance and dulled the mirrored reflections of the golden birch trees that lined the opposite shore.

Why couldn't he get her out of his mind and treat this like any other case? Sure, they had a history, but that was years ago. And people changed. Why hadn't he seen this side of her and refused to get involved with her again? Now his job was on the line.

They'd lived together that last year of school. Funny, he could remember that cramped one-room apartment like it was yesterday. The peeling green paint and the sagging maroon couch that made into a bed. Their passionate love-making on it. It's one window, and if you stood to one side and craned your neck, you could see the downtown lights at night. They had stood there the night before their graduation, her slender body leaning into his broad frame, locked in each other's arms. Starry-eyed about their future. He'd gotten a job with a law firm in Minneapolis and she'd gone with a hotel chain in Rochester, Minnesota. She began to travel for her company and gradually time and distance took a toll on their once sound relationship, finally resulting in closure. He'd heard she'd married. He'd come close once. When the woman had canceled out as the approaching date came closer, he found he'd been relieved. He'd practiced law in the city for years and then left for the ranch he'd inherited from his parents, and worked out of his home office in the country. He was successful and his business grew. But after years of hard work, he'd decided he had enough money and abruptly sold his ranch and business and semi-retired to his lake place, not even taking the time to let his friends know of his quick move.

The time flew by as he renovated the old cabin at the lake. The same one, he and Lindy had spent many week-ends at in college. He spent his time fishing, or on special assignments; investigating suspicious insurance claims.

He'd been stunned when Lindy Lewis's name had appeared on a sheet requiring his attention. She'd received a million dollars after a fire had destroyed her home, but new evidence had brought about further investigation. Reed found she was dating a man who went by the initials J.T. He had also been checking up on a new employee called Jud Thurman at his insurance company. Reed did not get suspicious until he'd requested all Tanner's records and he found the ear-marked file about John Thomas, the man Tanner had sent to prison years ago. The pieces began to fit together. Reed took another drink of his coffee.

It began two years ago, when his friend Tanner Burke had come to his office. Sierra had just been killed. The police ruled it accidental and closed the case, but Tanner would not accept that. A red car had been spotted in the area. Tanner had been absolutely convinced she'd been forced off the road into the deep ravine, by someone that had a vendetta against him. Then Tanner had been killed and it involved two men in a red car. The red car again!

When escaped convict John Thomas's fingerprints matched Jud Thurman's, the employee from Reed's Federated Insurance Company--the case had blown wide open! When he found out J.T. was Lindy's boyfriend, he knew it meant trouble.

Tanner Burke had been up North, in their home town when he'd been killed. Reed gripped the arms of his chair now as he sat at his desk in his office and remembered John Thomas's capture and the trial. Remembered how he'd had to grip himself from jumping up and choking the last breath out of the bastard as he'd bragged about his actions, but finally they'd put him back behind bars.

Reed took another drink of his coffee. Now the boss said "Find that woman!"

But where the hell was she?

-13-

The sign on the door said Pug Harris, Private Investigator. Lindy knocked and walked into the office again after hiring him a week ago. The cramped room held a desk, two straight backed chairs, and a dying ficus tree. A picture of a skeleton of a longhorn cow's head amidst sagebrush and sand hung on one of the yellowed walls.

Pug Harris was a barreled-chested big man in his fifties. His white hair accentuated by his craggy tanned face. His eyes were brown with deep lines bordering their edges. Lindy took a chair and sat down anxiously waiting to hear why he'd called her.

"Sorry to get you here so early," he said as he pushed a pile of papers over to the side of his desk.

Lindy gripped the edge of the chair and whispered in anticipation, "Have you found my car?"

"No, I'm sorry Miss Lewis, your car has disappeared. It's not anywhere in town!"

"But it's got to be!" Lindy stood up as frustrated tears threatened to start. "Mr. Harris, you don't understand, I need to find it!"

"I know that and I've got connections, Miss Lewis, but I haven't found a thing," Harris answered gruffly. He moved some papers again on his desk and stood up too.

"But where could it be?" Lindy's voice shook as she slumped back down in the chair.

"Miss Lewis, can't you turn it into your insurance company and get another one," Harris asked with a slight trace of impatience in his voice.

"I will have to soon I guess, but not yet." Lindy's face was forlorn.

"Miss Lewis, it's only a car." Of course, she hadn't told him the real reason she needed to find the car.

"Can you keep looking, Mr. Harris. Don't you have any more ideas?"

"Well, if you insist on spending more of your money, I can look forever."

"Please Mr. Harris," Lindy begged.

"Okay, I do have another idea, but I can't promise anything," he hastened to add.

"What?" Lindy's hope returned.

"It's just an inkling. I'll work on it and get in touch with you as soon as I get something to go on." As Lindy left the office, he shook his head at her insistence on continuing the search. But, what the hell, business was slow and rent was coming up. He reached for the phone and punched a number and Lindy went back to her motel room hopeful again.

The phone rang as she closed the door and her eyes lit up as Dade Lampart's familiar voice came over the line. "Lindy," he said, "I'm going to pick you up and take you for a ride. I promise to get you back in time for work." Sitting down in the sagging arm chair, Lindy drew an excited breath and whispered, "That sounds wonderful Dade!"

"Great Lindy, I'll be there in thirty minutes."

As the connection broke, Lindy couldn't help but be curious about Dade's persistence. They'd been out to dinner several times and he'd stop in at her restaurant for a drink often. They'd danced and seen a movie, but their dates always ended with a chaste kiss. Nothing more. Although Lindy was holding back on getting intimately involved, she still felt slightly rebuffed because of his lack of further actions.

She dressed in a new taupe wool long skirt and a matching over-blouse cinched at the waist with a gold chain belt. New brown calfskin boots and shoulder bag accentuated her dress. Her brunette hair had grown longer and looked chic swept up and caught with a gold comb. Chunky pewter jewelry completed her look. She stepped back and viewed herself in the mirror on the closet door. Not bad, she murmured satisfied. Just then Dade arrived.

"Wow, what a knockout," he winked as he eyed her up and down. He stood in the door and leaned against the doorway.

Not quite used to his outspoken flattery, Lindy's face suddenly felt warm. "You're not so bad yourself," she said shyly as she took in his brown snake-skinned boots, faded but sharp creased jeans and leather jacket. Without a hat tonight; his graying hair fell softly in waves around his head. And those gorgeous blue eyes. Lindy shivered inwardly as she gathered her purse and retrieved her keys from under the cushion of one of the sitting chairs.

The Texas sunshine was hot, the air humid as they stepped out of the motel. He helped her into a shiny maroon Lexus standing at the curb. Soon the air conditioner hummed softly and the sounds of classical music filled the inside of the luxurious car as they sped out of town.

Could there be a future for her with him, Lindy wondered? Oh, what was she thinking? After her disastrous affair with J.T. she didn't trust easily. Her marriage had been a security more in companionship than money, and she swore if she ever married again it would be for money first. Lindy leaned her head back against the leather headrest, lost in the music and her thoughts. This man could offer her security and a respected place in the community.

"Penny for your thoughts," Dade's voice brought her back. He reached over for her hand.

Sitting up, Lindy replied smoothly, "I'm just thinking how great it is to have the day off and to be heading out of town. I'm curious though, where are we going?"

"I'm taking you out to my ranch Lindy; I want you to see the place."

After they left the city the car purred along smoothly as heat shimmered in waves over the tarred highway. The landscape was beautifully overgrown with oak and pine trees, windblown mesquite and cactus. About thirty minutes later, Dade slowed down at a crossing and they turned under an archway that had Silver Dollar in black wrought iron letters across the top. Old gnarled oak trees lined the winding road, touching overhead, leading them through a green tunnel. White fences lined the road and crawled as far as the eye could see on both sides. Palomino horses and Hereford cattle grazed lazily in the pastures.

Lindy sucked in her breath as they rolled up to the house. A red bricked mansion sprawled smartly on the manicured lawn, gleaming in the morning sun. Off to the side, a patio filled with green and white striped furniture sat in groups around an Olympic sized pool. Perfectly groomed flowerbeds and shrubs graced the landscape. Magnolia trees and bougainvillea bushes draped lazily over the white fences.

"Dade, it's beautiful!" Lindy murmured awe-struck.

"Yep, it's my paradise. But, it takes a lot of work."

She asked curiously. "Do you live here alone?" They were standing by the car. He took her hand and pulled her along with him up to the door.

"Yes, I do, except for the Ortega's. They've been here for years. Sara takes care of the house and Sam the outside. They have their own place over in the orchard. He pointed to a neat little house nestled in a grove of apple trees. "Come on, let's go in and see what Sara has made for lunch.

A bronze statue of a stallion raised on his hind legs stood beside the bricked steps that led up to bright red double doors. Lindy was silent as she looked around at the beauty of Dade's home. Momentarily feeling out of her element, she wondered, why was this man who apparently had everything pursuing her? Certainly, he could have his pick of hundreds of Texas beauties!

-14-

I n a Kansas prison, a man in an orange coverall sat at a computer. As a genius at the keyboard, he had a plan. It had been over three months since his incarceration. I'll find that bitch, Lindy Lewis yet, he mumbled as he scanned the Internet. And that asshole Conners, his days are numbered. John Thomas smirked. A buzzer shrilled as the cell doors clanked open. He had two minutes to pass though inspection and get back to his cell.

***

"Will I see you later?" the cocktail waitress at Savard's Bar and Restaurant asked as she put a shot of whiskey down on the bar for Reed. It was a popular place in his small familiar town.

"I'll see how the night goes," Reed answered evasively. He took a sip of his drink, and tried not to take notice of the hurt in her voice. Ginger

Adams, lived in Reed's town in the north, was a long time friend and sometimes bed-partner. But since Lindy Lewis had popped back in his life; Reed had been treating her shabbily. Even he felt remorseful about his attitude. Tonight his two hundred pound frame slumped, the lines on his face deep as his eyes stared off into space.

"Have you been out on the water lately?" Ginger asked trying to make conversation. She stacked used glasses on the bar and loaded her tray with another order.

"Huh? Oh some," Reed answered absently. She had black hair, blue eyes and slim hips. She was hell in bed.

Goddamn! He said under his breath and thought, why do I let Lindy do this to me?

It had started years ago when she'd call and turn up for a few days, get him all charged and then nothing. Finally after being left hanging too many times, he'd buried himself in his work and put her out of his mind. He'd heard later that she'd married.

He'd known her for more than twenty-five years and sometimes got some scary intuitive feelings about her. Like that one time he'd been sitting in his office, hadn't heard from her for years and had known before he picked up his mail that day, there would be a letter from her. And there was! She'd gotten a promotion and was on her way to a big career. Then a few years ago, he'd felt a curious need to buy her hometown paper. A small publication, typical of rural areas with gossip, recipes and school activities. There on the second page was an announcement of Lindy's husband's death. He'd thought about contacting her then, but it had been so long, and she had her own life and friends. He didn't want to interfere. Later, he couldn't believe it when her name had come up in the insurance fraud.

What had happened to make her commit a crime of arson? Now Reed was counting on his intuition again to find her. He knew she had started working for a chain of hotels in Rochester; then moved around the country living in the south, sometimes in Atlanta and Dallas. She'd come back to Minnesota, married and stayed. In one of her infrequent letters, he remembered how she had said she'd fallen in love with the charm of the south.

Could that be where she'd gone? Then in his gut, suddenly he knew.

Reed stood up with a start, threw some bills on the bar and left without a backward glance at Ginger. He got into his car and put the key in the ignition.

Sometimes you're a damn fool, old man, he muttered. He slammed his fist on the steering wheel and started the Corvette. He stared out at the shaded grove of trees bordering the parking lot of Savard's. The engine purred into action, but still he sat. He turned on the CD player and light jazz played. He leaned back into the headrest and the romantic scent of late blooming heather came in through the open car window. He remembered the time he'd seen Lindy, that night she'd come into the casino and he'd seen the fear in her eyes. Heard the desperation in her voice when they'd talked, sitting together in the coffee shop. She still looked the same. The years had been kind to her. Although now her auburn hair was cut short and had a tousled look. Her cornflower blue eyes had a few fine lines around the edges, but only added character to her heart-shaped face. He could always read her pretty well by her eyes.

What had driven her to commit a crime? She'd always been a sweet kid. Hard working and honest. But then it had been more than two decades since they'd been together for any length of time. And people change. Arsonists set fires for peculiar reasons, deep seeded, sometimes not related to the actual deed.

Reed sat in his car, his gaze lost in the star-filled sky. It was a late fall night. A gentle breeze sent leaves falling silently like soft rain. The music, a slow sensuous song from the sixties purred from the sound system. He sat up and slammed his fist on the steering wheel again.

Goddamn, he had a restlessness eating at him. The same feeling he'd get every few years at this time, and then he and Tanner would plan a trip to hunt elk in Montana or fish in Canada. Now his friend was dead and soon the snow would fly.

When winter set in earnest, would he be content to stay at home with his books and a warm fire?

Hell, he muttered, he was going to Texas! He would find and capture arsonist Lindy Lewis and get his company's damn million dollars back, to end all this bullshit for good!

-15-

The next morning, Lindy sat holding her diamond and ruby earrings, which she'd retrieved from the pawn-broker. Deep in thought about the day before at Dade's house when they'd lingered over coffee and cordials in the living room. Then after lunch while they were close together on a couch, Dade leaned in and kissed her. Much to Lindy's surprise, a real kiss and on her lips! At the time she'd wondered how far things would go. Could it possibly heat up to an afternoon of love-making? By now, she was ready. But to her frustration, he'd released her and got up and began to pace around the room.

"Lindy, we've got to talk!" He stopped in front of her and pulled her to her feet. "But right now I've got to get you back to town like I promised."

A frown crossed Lindy's face as she wondered, what did Dade have in mind?

Bone-tired after another busy night at work and unable to sleep, she sat in her terry-cloth robe and sipped coffee from a cup she'd taken from the restaurant. A white flowered china cup and saucer. It was the only pretty thing in the room. The morning sun caught the dust motes lazily dancing over the worn carpet. An outfit that she'd worn lay over the arm of the old stuffed chair. She put her feet under herself and sat absorbed in her thoughts, the diamond earrings in one hand and the china cup in the other. After seeing the luxury of Dade's surroundings, hers looked pretty dismal. Today the ugliness of the room in the motel, a couple of decent outfits of clothes, and a killing job, far away from anything familiar was a piquant reminder of her life. When she'd lived and worked in Dallas years before, things were altogether different. Of course then, she'd been young and full of dreams.

She pulled the robe closer around herself. It was fall, with a slight chill in the air. Although the south had a warmer autumn than the north, she missed the rich aroma of the ripe vegetation from the mossy black earth, and smoke from burning leaves.

Chilled, Lindy went over to the bed and got in. She pulled the covers up to her chin and continued to worry.

What'll I do if I can't find my money? I just can't stay here and float along without a plan.

Could there be a future for her with Dade? Maybe, but something about him caused an uneasy feeling in her. Suddenly loneliness overwhelmed her. She started to cry. First whimpering sobs, then angry cursing tears that burned her throat. She beat the pillow in her anguish, damming the man that had stolen all she had in the world, then curled into a fetal position and clutched the blankets around her and fell asleep. Or maybe just into that early stage of slumber of shadows and gray dreams.

She was small again; a little girl on a run-down farm miles away from the city. Barefoot, in a ragged dress and a braid down her thin back. A cry of anguish erupted from the six year old girl, used and ravished by a relative and not knowing where to go to find safety. She remembered running, trying to hide. Finally, she got a reprieve and her parents sent her away to school. She was free! She worked and saved her money for college, and soon was working on a degree in business. Amidst studies and part-time jobs, she met a young man. A handsome cook in a greasy spoon cafe they both worked at. His name was Reed Conners. They were in their early twenties and it was1971. Elvis, the Beatles and bell-bottom pants were all the rage. Head-bands, platform shoes and peace signs were everywhere. For the first time, Lindy felt an attraction to a man.

Warmed, Lindy threw the blankets off and turned over in her sleep. A smile touched the corners of her lips. Drifting again, she felt the same warmth in her house, in her cozy kitchen with the round oak table and chairs by the wide windows and a pot of stew simmering on the stove; awaiting her husband's arrival from work.

Lindy took a deep breath in her sleep relishing the zesty aroma. Oh that house, even now in Lindy's dream it stood proudly atop the hill. She'd met and married a hard working man and the years spread before her in a panoramic flow of their happy years of being together and fixing it up. It was a seventy-five year old mansion standing in a valley surrounded by rolling hills. Later a housing development came in, but then they were gloriously alone in all the beauty. It was a two story colonial. A veranda ran along three sides of the building with columns set along the edges. It was in foreclosure for back taxes and had been standing abandoned for years. The minute, Lindy and her husband walked in, she had felt warmth amongst the faded walls and creaking floors. This was what she wanted. She felt safe.

Years went by, as they tore down, refinished, painted and gradually made it into a beauty. Their bodies ached, their hands bled, but finally it was done. Their palatial house stood finished in all its glory. Now a moan escaped Lindy's lips as she dreamed. As she remembered, "It's cancer," the Doctor had told her husband. Then the inevitable silence in the house later when she was alone. The silence that never went away.

She hugged herself, twisted in the flimsy blankets. She turned her face into the pillow. A tremor shook her body as a look of desperation crossed her face. She'd been seeing small piles of sawdust around the house from time to time. Strange, but not anything she took seriously. There would be some on top of a dresser in an upstairs bedroom, or downstairs on a kitchen counter. This went on for several months.

This seems to be falling out of the ceiling, Lindy muttered one day as she was cleaning house. What the hell is it? She tied her flannel shirt up in a knot, wiped her forehead on her sleeve as she looked to the top of the room in bewilderment. In a corner a small crack was visible. She went through the rest of the house and found small cracks appeared in most of the ceilings.

Damn, Lindy said under her breath, what was happening to her beautiful house?   Was something going on in the attic? Leaving her rags, bottles and cans of cleaning supplies in the middle of the living room, she marched purposely into the back hallway to an attic door with a pull-down ladder. She yanked it down with the attached handle in an agitated huff. She'd never been up there--never wanted to. But now she didn't have a choice. Her knees were shaking as she climbed, grasping the steps ahead. Finally she was eye level with the attic floor. As her eyes began to adjust to the gloom, she gasped at the ugliness of the huge cavern. Spider webs like glistening patterns of lace hung from the rafters adorning the walls, settling into the mounds of gray insulation.

Lindy stood grasping the attic floor, horrified as something crawled over her hand. She jerked backwards, her foot slipped and the top ladder step creaked. As she hung on and regained her balance her hand moved some of the insulation on the floor and then she saw them. Huge black carpenter ants embedded in the boards, busily eating away. She didn't remember climbing down the ladder, only the thunderous bang as she pushed the ladder back up to the ceiling and it snapped into place. She ran outside, shaking violently. Later that week, an exterminator had shook his head and jokingly said, "Lady, you better burn this joint!"

-16-

The afternoon before, when Dade had opened the door and led Lindy into his home she had thought, my God, my house was big but I could have fit it into one wing of this place! Hardwood floors gleamed in the large foyer and a round mahogany gate-legged table stood in the middle of the room with a huge centerpiece of fall flowers. From the ceiling, a brilliant hanging crystal chandelier sent prisms of dancing light down over yellows, rusts and creams of the bouquet. He had led her through a sitting room done in creams and beiges. Davenports and stuffed chairs set in groups through out the room. Soft rugs were scattered in each setting.

"Here's my favorite place," he said stepping into another wing of the house. This was a man's room. Caramel leather furniture and shelves of books lined the walls. Soft cream carpet covered the floor. "Here, sit down. I see Sarah has chilled a bottle of champagne." Lindy sank into the satiny leather chair. The room had a woodsy smell from the fireplace.

Trying to appear relaxed, Lindy's mind hadn't been still. *I could have luxury like this too, if I had my money!* The familiar hopeless feeling washed over her again that someone else had what was hers. But, --maybe not, she consoled herself. Her eyes had a faraway look in them as she thought for a minute, that stop in Oklahoma City had been a smart idea. Her craft with a needle and thread had come in handy as she had painstakingly sewn her fortune into the backrest of the passenger seat in her BMW. She put a smile back on her face as Dade turned from the bar and handed her a crystal flute.

Lindy took a sip of the champagne and wrinkled her nose as the bubbles burst and tickled. "Have you always lived here," she asked Dade as he leaned against the bar that was tucked into an alcove across the room.

"I was born and raised here. My Granddaddy started the place, and then my Dad took over. He died four years ago and then my mother went."

"I'm sorry." Lindy took another sip of her champagne thinking, *you can't feel too sorry for someone who's left with all this, though can you?* "You must have a lot of cattle out here?" She smiled at him and wondered how much a cow was worth.

Dade walked over and sat across from Lindy in another matching leather chair. "Yes, I raise beef cattle and Palomino horses.

Lindy had sat demurely and made pleasant conversation. "I didn't see any neighbors; don't you get lonesome way out here?" she asked.

"There aren't any. I bought up all the land for hundreds of miles around here." Dade had a satisfied look on his face as he answered.

"Why?" Lindy asked curiously.

Dade smiled. For a second a steely gleam flashed through his eyes, "Because I wanted to get rid of the trash." Lindy took another drink of her champagne and looked away. An uneasy feeling darted across her chest. Dade refilled their glasses. Restless now, Lindy got up and walked over to the large patio door and looked out. The view was breathtaking. A plush green lawn sloped down to a pond bordered on the opposite side with birch and pine trees. Ducks swam lazily around in the softly rippling water. Just then Sarah Ortega came in. A Spanish woman; short, stout and flushed.

"Mr. Lampart, I have lunch set in the morning room for you and your guest. It is ready now," she said backing out of the room. Dade picked up their glasses.

"Come, Sarah is the best cook in Texas."   The meal was sumptuous. Lindy had eaten with relish after the champagne had relaxed the knots in her stomach. She looked around with interest and couldn't help wondering how it would feel living here and being a part of this kind of life. She wouldn't need to worry about where her money was!

Dade wondered if she would fit in. The booming voice of his attorney still vibrated in his ears at last night's meeting.

"Dadelyn my boy," he'd said, "you've got until the first of the year to straighten out your life. Give up the boyfriend and find a wife, or according to your Daddy's will, you're out without a cent!"

Dade smiled at Lindy.

-17-

"Do you have to go?"

"Now Johnny, you know Mama has to work. You can go next-door to Merna's at five o'clock and have supper there. When you come home, be sure and lock the door before you go to bed. I don't want someone coming in and stealing anything."

Mrs. Thomas busily applied her make-up as the eight-year-old boy sat on her bed. Angry voices from the apartment upstairs echoed through the thin floors. Young John Thomas stayed alone when his mother worked. He'd grown used to being scared and sometimes looked for safety in his mother's room. The flowers on the faded wallpaper and the cheap pink rug reminded him of the softness he'd once seen in a picture of a family. He'd go in and just sit. He'd hold her perfume bottles and touch her jewelry. Always careful to put her things back in the exact same place.

He loved his mother, but was lonely and didn't remember not being so. He'd never seen his father, but was sure he had one. One time he'd been looking in his mother's dresser drawers and in the one on the bottom that was full of papers, he'd found a picture. A man dressed in jeans and a plaid shirt stood with his arms around his mother. He had brown curly hair and dark brown eyes. Johnny saw something familiar about the man, not realizing he was looking at the exact reflection of himself. He'd kept the picture hidden in his room for days and studied it when he was alone. Finally one day he mustered up enough courage to ask about it.

"Mama, is this my Daddy?" His little hand shook as he held it out for her to see.

"Johnny, where did you get that?" His mother sat at the chipped wood kitchen table painting her nails and smoking a cigarette. Her flowered housecoat washed out and rumpled. Dyed black hair hung uncombed around her lined face. Dirty dishes were piled on the cupboards and filled the sink.

"You've been snooping in my things again, haven't you?" She reached over and snatched it out of his hand and stuffed it into her robe pocket. A slap cracked across his face and echoed in the room. Johnny pulled back. Tears fell down his cheeks.

"But I didn't mean to, Mama." Why does she always hit me, his small mind wondered? She always seemed to be mad. Sometime later, he was awakened in the night by a commotion coming from her bedroom. Getting up quietly, he crept out of his bed and opened the door of her room. He saw a man on top of his mother in her bed.

"Mama," he cried out, wanting to protect her from harm. He flew into the room and jumped on the man's back, hitting and kicking as hard as his small limbs could manage.

"Jesus Christ, what the hell?" The naked man caught Johnny and threw him on the floor. Mrs. Thomas grabbed a blanket and covered herself and sat up.

"Johnny, how many times have I told you never to come in my room? Now go back to bed!" Shamefaced, he got up on trembling legs and went into his room. Now he knew what they were doing. Now he remembered those pictures his friend had shown him. It was called fucking, he'd said. A lock appeared on his mother's bedroom door after that. As he grew over the years, seeing the parade of men and hearing the noises in her bedroom, he realized she was a prostitute. He hated her. He hated everything. When he was fourteen, he ran away from home, much to his mother's relief he was sure. His perception of women was that they were all whores, and only a means of making money for you. Some way, somehow. Years later, as he sat in the Kansas prison, the computer hummed. John Thomas was onto something.

-18-

Reed Conners threw his leather bag in the back of his Corvette and hit the road. Mirrored aviator glasses sat low on the bridge of his nose. It was six A.M. The sky overcast. Rain tinged with snow began to slide over the windshield as he turned from the gravel road onto the interstate. He had sat at his desk late into the night and studied the files again from the insurance company. Everything fit together in a neat package. Everything except Lindy's whereabouts. He had to find her!

The freeway was quiet this early in the morning; although with the drizzle and dropping temperatures a layer of ice would cover it soon. Country music soothed Reed's frayed nerves as he drove, lost in his thoughts, intent on his plans. He figured it would take him three days to get to Dallas. To the suburb called Flower Mound. Lindy had lived there years ago and had a friend in the city. Mitzi Grover, a nurse. Reed had met her once. She'd come along with Lindy when they spent a week up at his cabin. He'd also done some work for Mitzi to collect child support payments from her ex-husband. But would Mitzi still be there?

Now the rain had turned to snow and the landscape began to take on a fairyland look. Traffic picked up as he got closer to Minneapolis, but after a quick stop for breakfast Reed was again heading south. The sun began to shine as he drove through Iowa. Here the farmers were harvesting their cornfields and the temperatures began to rise. When it got dark he stopped at a motel. The next morning, after eight hours of sleep, he slipped a CD on the player and settled into good music. The miles flew by as he drove the low slung car, now almost an extension of himself. When he got to Dallas, he'd try the old telephone number he had of Mitzi's from years ago. Being a nurse and having a child he didn't think she'd be apt to go too far from her roots.

In Kansas, he stopped for a cup of coffee. Here the scenery was dry and bare on the prairies. Reed Conners had always been a loner, but now he wished he had someone to share this beauty with. Another night drew near and Reed stopped at a motel. He had just crossed over into Oklahoma. He stretched his stiff back as he got out of the car. The sky was jet black with a million stars and the temperature a balmy eighty degrees. Oil wells dotted the landscape as far as the eye could see. A fascinating world to Reed, only he preferred the laid-back country warmth of the north. The next morning he was on the last stretch of his journey and by late afternoon, he was in Texas where the temperature was in the nineties. Herds of longhorn cattle grazed lazily in the green pastures. A sign ahead said, Flower Mound-- five miles.

"I don't know how long, a few weeks at least." Reed stood at the counter of the Wagon Wheel Inn and signed the registration. After unpacking, he sat down on the bed and dialed Mitzi Grover's telephone number. Just as he feared, that number had been disconnected and Dallas had no listing for her.

"Bernard," he said into the telephone after checking his phone book, "Plug in that computer of yours, I need to find someone."

"Reed, what the hell are you up to? Where are you?"

"I'm in the south; I need you to find a female. Mitzi Grover, a nurse licensed in Texas. Here's her social security number."

"How long ago?"

"Back fifteen years maybe."

"Jesus--Conners, she could be dead by now. Hell, give me a couple hours."

"Also will you check the DMV?"

"It'll cost you!"

"Yeah, yeah, I'll call you at ten." Reed left his room and headed over to a coffee shop just across the street called Shonney's. A whiff of greasy French fries teased his hunger pangs as he found a booth. The place had a cozy feeling. Flowered fabric on the chair backs matched the valances over the mini-blinds that covered the windowed walls. The place reminded him of home. He lit a cigarette and put some coins in the tableside music machine. There were two kinds of music, he noticed--country and jazz. He chose Garth Brooks and settled in with the Dallas paper to see what was happening in Texas.

"Hello handsome," a cute brunette waitress drawled as she came over. "What'll you have?"

Reed looked up. "A steak sandwich and some fries, I guess."

"Do you want a cold beer to wash that down?"

"Sounds good." Her nametag said Betty. She had an inviting sway to her hips as she walked away. Nice legs too, Reed noticed.

"Are you new around here?" she asked as she placed his food in front of him a few minutes later.

"Just got into town." Reed flushed under her open gaze.

"Where are you from?" she continued.

"Minnesota."

"Well, welcome to the south. I'll leave you so you can eat." She looked to be in her forties and had an easy smile.

"So what do you do when you're not working, Betty?" Reed asked when she came back to his table later.

"I wish I could say nothing. I've got two kids to support and I work another job."

"Wow that takes a lot of energy." Reed got up from the booth and reached for his billfold to pay for his meal.

"What's your second job? I hope it's one sitting down."

"No, it's the same. Soon as I finish up here, I head over to Tony's and work the late dinner shift." They walked together to the cashier's desk. "You must have seen the signs. They're plastered all along the highways. You know, *Visit Tony's Steakhouse for a Taste of Splendor*."

"Oh yeah, I do remember seeing them. I'll have to stop in and see you one night."

"Thanks handsome." Reed could feel her eyes following him as he went out the door. Back at his motel he called Bernard again.

"You're in luck Buddy. I've got an address on her."

"Where?"

"Here it is. 1620 Grant Street in North Dallas. This was several years ago though."

"Might work. Thanks Bern." He grabbed his keys and left the room. Lights were blinking around the city as Reed drove into Dallas. The freeways more crowded than ever.

Jesus, you've got to be nuts to live in this town, he muttered as he raced along going eighty-five miles an hour, just to keep up with the traffic. He stopped at a service station and checked his map. 1620 Grant was a three-story brick apartment building in a rundown part of town. Life sucks was written along with other negative graffiti on an old wood fence surrounding it. Someone's attempt to pretty up the place had failed dismally by the look of dried up rose bushes edging the cracked sidewalk. He parked and went in. There it was, M. Grover--Apartment number four.

But would she help him find Lindy? Reed ran a hand over his sandy hair as he walked up the stairs to the second floor. Cooking aromas mingled in the closed air; onions, tomatoes and garlic. The carpeted stairway was worn and dusty. A dog barked in one apartment. Foreign speaking voices raised in an argument in another as he climbed the stairs. Reed knocked on Apartment four. The place was quiet. He knocked again.

"Hold on," a man's voice said. Reed waited. "Yeah, what do you want?" The man had opened the door and looked at Reed with an impatient glare.

"Sorry to bother you. I'm looking for Mitzi Grover."

"Yeah, why?" A towel hung over his shoulders. Tousled brown hair hung wet and slick down his tanned face.

"My name is Reed Conners. Does Mitzi live here?"

"So what if she does." The man's voice cracked

"Sorry to barge in, but I would like to talk to Mitzi." Reed continued patiently.

"She's not here. What's your name again?"

"Reed Conners."

"Okay, we got that straight. Why do you want to see her?" He eyed Reed suspiciously.

Reed returned his stare. "May I come in?"

"Make it fast."

As Reed stepped into the living room, he gave it a practiced quick once over. It was furnished with rattan furniture in shades of brown, black and creams. A brass floor lamp glowed dimly against the dark night.

"Is Mitzi here?" Reed asked again.

"No, she's not!"

"I'd like to leave my number."

"Suit yourself."

A man of many words, Reed thought dryly. "She still a nurse?" For a minute, he'd been ready to punch the arrogant bastard.

"Ask her." The man walked away and left Reed standing.

Asshole! Reed muttered as he laid his card with the motel's number written on the back, on an end table and went back out the door.

Had Mitzi married this guy, he wondered? If she had, he didn't appear to be much better than her last husband. He had wanted to ask if Lindy had contacted them, but with the man's attitude was sure he'd never tell him anything. Reed got back into his Corvette and drove away, the whole night ahead of him now. He couldn't do anything until tomorrow, and that would all depend on whether Mitzi called him.

He drove along without any destination in mind other then to find a restaurant. Where was that place Betty had said she worked? A big Texas steak would hit the spot and after driving twenty minutes, he found the place. A large marquee sat atop the brick building and the parking lot was filled with expensive cars; Mercedes, Lincolns and Lexus's. Exhaust from the kitchen filled the parking lot with mouth-watering aromas of prime steaks and bread baking as Reed walked in.

"What'll you have?" a bartender asked him as he sat down at the bar.

"Whiskey, and then one of those steaks you advertise."

"You won't be disappointed. I'll call the hostess and have her get a table ready for you."

Reed savored the chilled drink and lit up a cigarette. When he found Lindy, what would he do first? Call the authorities and have her arrested, or listen to her story. His stomach hurt. But was it from hunger or the possibility of being so close? Goddamn, he muttered under his breath, she had played him for a fool! He had his job and the security of his company to think about. He'd find her, and settle this if it took the rest of his life.

-19-

Lindy awoke from her nightmare to the furiously ringing phone on the bedside table. She sat up and looked around in confusion. Her head ached and her throat was parched as she reached over to still the offending noise.

"Miss Lewis, Pug Harris here, can you stop in today?"

Awake now, Lindy's breath caught. "Have you found my car?"

"We'll talk when you come in," he said in his gruff voice.

"I'll be there shortly," Lindy said as she threw the blankets off and stood up. For a moment, the room spun. Last night's make-up was dried and caked on her face; her hair stood up in unruly tufts. She stepped into the shower not waiting for the water to warm. She had to clear her head. Forty minutes later she got out of the taxi and ran into the private investigator's office. Today Pug Harris's ruddy face was even brighter next to the red jacket he wore. His desk, still messy with files and papers scattered on the floor. Lindy sat, expectantly waiting for him to tell her something of importance. She'd thrown on the first thing she'd come across to wear and pulled the short skirt down to cover her knees. Car exhaust blew into the room from the open window as the early traffic crawled by outside.

"Mr. Harris, have you found my car?" Her eyes searched his face as he sat, elbows bent, leaning on his desk.

"Here's what I found, according to my connections, cars like yours are in big demand. They're stripped down and the parts are sent over the border. After they are repainted and the numbers changed--bingo, there's no way to trace them. Money changes hands fast in that business."

"Are you talking about chop shops?"

"I see you've heard of them."

"Well, you see it on TV. So you're saying it's gone for good, Mr. Harris?"

"It looks that way. I'm sorry."

Lindy got up from her chair and hopelessness sagged her shoulders. "Miss Lewis, call your insurance company and report it stolen."

"Yes, I'll have to do that." Lindy walked to the door. Her face, ashen.

"Course, it could have been some small time hood, just working on his own. Could be hidden in a garage somewhere, just waiting for the right time!"

"You mean--?"

"No, this is a big town. Sorry, there just isn't any more I can do for you." Pug Harris shook his head. "It's gone for good."

Lindy left his office and walked until she found a coffee shop, but her stomach rebelled. Leaving her food untouched, she caught a taxi again and went home. With her car gone for good and the money she'd hidden in it, what could she do?

The week went by as Lindy worked and fell into bed exhausted each night. She was depressed. But, one comment Pug Harris had made stuck in her mind. She took a cigarette from the pack she'd bought, lit one and coughed as she sat in one of the faded chairs in her motel room. Her thoughts settled again on an idea that had been swirling around in her head. When it was time to get ready for work, she knew what she would do.

"Yes, read that back to me please," Lindy asked the lady at the Dallas newspaper office the next morning.

"$10,000 dollars cash reward for the return of a black 2006 BMW, taken from 54th and Magnolia on September 6th. No questions asked. Contact Box 62A35. Dallas, Texas."

"Is that it?"

"Yes," Lindy answered. "But underline, no questions asked."

"And how long do you want this to run?"

"I'm not sure---, two weeks for now I guess."

That night as Lindy finished her shift and relaxed at the bar with a Manhattan, Dade walked in. He flashed a smile.

"I thought you'd gotten lost way out there in the prairie," Lindy said nonchalantly.

"I had to go out of town for a few days."

Not in a good mood, Lindy lit up a cigarette.

"Whoa, when did you start that?" He stood back out of the stream of smoke.

"Just a habit I pick up now and then."

"Lindy, do you have any plans for the week-end? I remember you said you had this one off." Dade sat down on the next bar stool. He wore a black western hat and a black leather jacket. The white turtle-neck sweater matched the gleaming white of his perfect teeth.

"Yes, I'm off for the weekend. Why?" she turned to him. Dade leaned over and put an arm over her shoulder.

"I'd like to invite you to come out to the ranch."

"Really, that sounds interesting." If she was going to spend the weekend, no doubt, that meant they'd sleep together. She looked at him again and curiously wondered what kind of lover he'd be.

"Great, I'll pick you up tomorrow after work. Bring some jeans for riding."

"I haven't been on a horse for years," Lindy laughed, "but I'll try."

"I've got to run. I'll see you tomorrow then." He stood up and kissed her on the cheek. Lindy continued to sit at the bar after he left. They had known each other two months now. A niggling thought crossed her mind. She liked to call it her bad witch complex. She couldn't help it as she smiled within.

What would marriage to a wealthy man be like? No more working and worrying over money. No sore feet and tired back. God, she sighed, it was so hard to be doing this kind of work again, after she'd given it up years ago. She sipped her Manhattan and puffed on her cigarette. Now, more than ever she had to find a way out of this mess.

But, did she like his money more than she liked him? Truthfully, Lindy guessed she did.

Friday night, Dade was there as she finished work. After they got on the road, Lindy checked her purse to make sure she'd brought along the little disk of birth control pills. The bad witch surfaced again for just an instant. Lindy blinked in surprise and had to stifle a giggle. Maybe she wouldn't take them this weekend! Outrageous high school thinking, she scolded herself as she settled into the plush seat. It was past midnight when they got to the ranch. Lights blazed from the house as they walked in.

"I'll show you to your bedroom, maybe you'll want to freshen up." Lindy followed Dade through the house and into another wing of the mansion. Here the carpet muffled their steps as they walked along. Doors stood open leading into sitting rooms with connecting bedrooms.

Would Dade put her in his bedroom? Lindy wondered. They stopped as he opened a set of double doors. Soft pink lights glowed across the cream carpet. White oak furniture filled the room. A king-sized bed stood under a canopy of lace. Beige pillows and afghans were tossed on a cream couch with matching chairs off in a corner. Paintings of Victorian garden scenes done in soft colors graced the walls. The room was gorgeous. Dade put her bag on a low bench as Lindy stepped in and looked around.

"My room is just through there," Dade said as he pointed to a connecting door. "Make yourself comfortable." Turning to leave he added, "Come to the library whenever you're ready, I'll chill some wine."

After the door closed, Lindy kicked off her shoes and buried her sore toes in the lush carpet. Going into the spacious bathroom, she ran a tub of water and helped herself to bubble bath from the assortment set on a shelf. With her hair pinned up on top of her head, she sank down into the soothing water. After a few minutes, she stuck one foot out of the water, pointed her toes and balanced a bubble. Soft music spiraled into the bathroom as Lindy relaxed in the perfumed water. Some time later, she stepped out onto heated floor tiles and dried off. She freshened her make-up and put on a new leopard print lounging set she'd bought at a boutique, along with high-heeled gold sandals. She fluffed her hair, finally satisfied with her appearance. Now she was ready to dazzle Dade. Lindy retraced her steps and found him in the library, sitting in a lounge chair, legs stretched out on an ottoman. Glass in hand.

"I hope I didn't take too long." She sat down in a matching chair next to his.

"You must be tired after working all night." He got up and went to the bar in the corner of the room and filled a crystal flute with champagne. Lindy sat back and took a sip.

"You look beautiful tonight, Lindy." Dade murmured. The music had switched to a classical tango. Lindy rested her head on the back of her chair and became immersed in her surroundings and the moment. Dade refilled their glasses. He reached over and took her hand a little later as they listened to the music and sipped the champagne.

"Lindy, what would you say to us getting married!" Lindy jerked her thoughts back to the present.

"What?" Her eyes grew large and her breath caught.

Dade got out of his chair and kneeled on the floor. He leaned towards her.

"I know this is sudden Lindy. But, when I make up my mind about something, I don't fool around with waiting!" He sat down on the floor and reached for his champagne.

Lindy was flabbergasted. Unable to think, she reached for her drink. The music flowed softly through hidden speakers. The flames in the fieldstone fireplace licked gently over the logs giving off a faint aroma of apples. Lindy hadn't expected this. Dreamed about it yes, but it was only that. A dream! She looked around at the luxurious room and thought of the grandeur of his lifestyle. It all looked awesome, but was she really ready for this, and him?

Dade sat on the floor by her chair. "I want to settle down with you Lindy." He looked deep into her eyes.

Lindy sipped her champagne as thoughts whirled around in her mind.

"We could have a good life together. I could give you anything you wanted," Dade continued.

Lindy smiled at him. Yes, he could!   The champagne welled up in her throat at that thought.

"Lindy, I want to get married before the New Year. A Christmas wedding. What do you think?" Dade reached over and turned her face to his.

"Dade," she stammered, "we haven't known each other that long. Shouldn't we wait awhile?"

"Lindy, we have all the time in the world to get to know each other." She sat quietly, suddenly the whole idea of marriage too vast an idea to grasp.

Finally, she said, "I'm flattered Dade. But, what about love?" Oh God, she thought sucking in her breath, maybe I said the wrong thing. Maybe I've blown my chances.

"Don't say anything more Lindy, just think about it. In the meantime, I've got something for you." Lindy looked at him uncertainly then smoothed her leopard pants leg and noted the polish on her toenails matched her fingertips perfectly. Curiously, she watched as he opened a small box. Then he picked up her left hand and slipped a ring on her finger. She looked down at a diamond as big as a marble and sat immobilized. He pulled her to her feet and took her in his arms.

"This is to help you think about it." He kissed her then, his cologne heavy in the air. Vince Gill's crooning voice came over the speaker as he sang a love song. Lindy stood on her tiptoes and gave him her lips. It turned into a deep kiss, with tongues entwined. He pressed her to him. His maleness hard against her. The champagne whirled in Lindy's head. Butterflies fluttered in her stomach as they danced in a tight embrace. Abruptly, Dade took the bottle of champagne, grabbed their glasses in one hand and led her out of the library and down the long hallway. At her bedroom door, he stopped and kicked it open.

"Let's make a toast to us," he said releasing her hand and refilling their glasses. Lindy's head spun. They drank, they danced and they kissed.

***

Some time later, Lindy eased herself out of bed. She put a shaking hand over her mouth to quiet her rasping breath. Her lips were bleeding and her body bruised. She searched frantically in the dark for her clothes, grabbed her purse and fled silently through the dark to the door. For the way out! She picked up Dade's car keys he'd tossed on the table in the foyer earlier, ran to his Lexus, pulled open the door and climbed in. The big diamond flashed in the dash light as she fumbled for the ignition. She got the car going and then didn't dare turn on the headlights until she was down the road. Tears cursed down her face.

When had his passion turned to abuse? As caught up as she had been in their lovemaking, when he'd trapped her arms above her head with one hand, she'd hesitated. She knew she was in trouble when he began hurting her, then no amount of struggling could stop him. Lindy shivered as she remembered her pleading had only seemed to excite him. She couldn't think about it now, she had to get away. Faraway from this man. Lindy drove the big luxurious car, holding back hysterical sobs. She couldn't fall apart now; she needed to find her way back to town and get to the safety of her room.

The spicy, moldy smell of drying sagebrush came through the air vent and the silence, eerie as the wind whistled. When she came to a crossroads she recognized the area and with relief remembered the way back. The city lights came into view, and thank God, 5th and Magnolia was just a few miles away. Leaving the keys in the car, Lindy ran into the safety of her room. Bolting the door, she tore off her clothes and turned on the shower. She washed and scrubbed her throbbing body. Then scrubbed again. She had to get rid of his taste, his smell, his touch and the hurt.

Realizing the shower had run cold; Lindy stepped out and wrapped in a towel. Shivering, she looked at herself in the mirror. Her hair hung in wet strands. Remnants of mascara smeared her ghostly white face. All her confidence was gone. Her hopes and dreams forgotten. She was twelve years old again, lost and alone. Her sobs burst out, uncontrolled and frightening. When she fell on her bed it was five in the morning. The moonlight shining through the motel window suddenly dimmed and a deafening clap of thunder shook the room. She huddled in the covers as the storm began to rage outside the motel and dampness crept in through the thin walls. Finally, hours later, as the storm passed overhead, Lindy threw the covers off. Now she was angry!

She'd been raped! Just like years ago, but then she'd been a little girl and couldn't do anything about it. She'd go to the police! She'd get him, put him in jail. Sitting wrapped in a blanket with her hair straight and lank, her face still swollen from her tears. She felt justified at last as she whispered, "Dade Lampart, you won't get away with this!"

The long weekend loomed ahead of her. Maybe she'd call Mitzi Grover. She needed a friend. A few years had gone by since they'd talked, and Mitzi lived in the same suburb, Flower Mound. They met in college and had known each other for over twenty years. She reached for the phone and waited anxiously for Mitzi's voice to come over the line. But after eight rings, she had to hang up. Disappointed now that she hadn't called before and told Mitzi she was in town. But she didn't want to involve Mitzi in case of trouble. Her thoughts went back to Dade. She began to feel like a fool for falling for his charms; his money and lifestyle. Brushing her hair out of her eyes, her breath caught. Could she be wrong? Had she led him on and just imagined his actions?

She got up out of her chair and peeked through the blinds. His maroon Lexus still stood outside her motel door and was parked sideways, just as she'd left it last night after she raced back to her room. Would Dade show up soon to pick it up? Then thought maybe the same thief that stole my car will come back and take his too!

As she sat, lonely and depressed, she suddenly remembered the ring and looked down at her hand. The finger on her left hand was empty! Oh God, had she carelessly tossed it somewhere while driving back to the city last night, maybe out the window? She hardly remembered the wild ride, only standing in the shower with the water washing over her and soothing her bruised body. Her eyes darted around the room. Had she dropped it somewhere? She crawled on her hands and knees, looking under the chairs and the bed as her heart raced. She hurried into the bathroom and threw back the shower curtain. There winking at her, caught on the screen in the drain, lay the diamond ring. She picked it up and held it up to the light, moving it side to side in the sunlight. She slipped it on her finger and watched as it sparkled, then laid it on a table. Longingly she thought--, it would have looked good on her hand. Big and expensive.

It was nine o'clock on Saturday morning. Feeling wretched from loss of sleep, faint from stress and hunger, Lindy pulled on jeans and a sweater. She needed food and someone to talk to. She hastily applied make-up and curled her hair. Dressed now, her bruises were covered. She put the ring in her jean pocket as she walked outside to the coffee shop across the street. Lindy greeted the waitress as she slid into a booth in a corner.

"Would you like some coffee?" Betty the waitress asked.

"I need some," Lindy replied and tried to smile. The room bustled with breakfast customers and the air was laced with bacon frying on the grill and hot maple syrup. She held the steaming cup in her hands a few minutes later and began to sip the rich brew.   "When you have time, would you bring me some eggs and toast please?" she asked.

"Just give me a few minutes sweetie, the whole town decided to come to Shonneys today." Betty laughed good naturedly and disappeared in the kitchen. Lindy rummaged in her purse for her cigarettes as she waited for her food, then sat still in a stupor after last nights events. Betty refilled her coffee.

Lindy liked her and needing a friend said "When you have a break, why don't you join me Betty?"

"Why I'd love to, ten minutes? Reinforcements are on the way."

Betty was a few years older, a single parent, with two teen-aged boys. She worked two jobs; days' here at Shoney's coffee shop and then nights at Tony's Steakhouse. She was like a mother to everyone, and she'd been especially nice to Lindy when she'd started working at the same restaurant.

"Betty, how do you do it, working two jobs?" Lindy asked as they sat together in a corner booth.

She had grinned, "Sometimes I wonder. Between aches and pains and the boys needing something extra." She sipped her coffee and lit a cigarette. "Honey, you look like hell. Are you all right?"

"No--, I didn't sleep last night." Lindy took a deep breath. Betty didn't say anything for a minute. Just sat there studying her. "I saw you leave with

Dade Lampart last night. I take it things didn't go
so well!"   Lindy's hand shook as she lifted her cup
of coffee to her lips and winched as the hot liquid
touched her lips. She put the cup down, steadied it
with both hands.

"Listen honey," Betty said softly "I've been
around this town all my life, if you want to girl-
talk. Anything you want to say, I've probably been
there and done it." She smiled openly. "I liked you
right from the start, when you started working at
Tony's."

Lindy smiled weakly, grateful to have someone
to talk to. "Betty," she said out of trembling lips,
"What do you know about Dade?"

Betty gave a harsh laugh. "Do you really want
to know?"

Lindy sat back in the booth. "How well do you
know him?"

"Honey, I've known Dade Lampart for years."

"How do you know him, did you ever go out
with him?"

"No," Betty laughed, "he travels in different
circles. I've seen him romancing you lately."

"Betty, I've got to talk to someone." Lindy
swallowed and went on, "We've been seeing each
other for almost two months now and he invited
me out to his ranch for the weekend"

Betty eyed her expectantly. "Yes, go on."

"Oh God," Lindy whispered and took a shaking breath. "First he proposed to me and then," Lindy leaned close and whispered, "he raped me!"

"He raped you?" Betty reached over and clasped her hand, "Oh God Lindy, I'm sorry. Did you go to the hospital?"

"No--, I'm okay."

"That ass-hole! I can't believe it. Lord, I wondered how long it would be before he showed his true colors."

"What do you mean?" Lindy clutched her cup of coffee.

"Oh sweetie, I guess I'm going to be the one to have to tell you, its rumored Dade Lampart is gay!"

"What?" Lindy's cup of coffee dropped out of her hand and splashed across the tabletop. She gaped at her friend. "You mean he goes with men?"

"That's what we've heard. I guess he thought he could hide it from you." Betty mopped up the spilled coffee with napkins.

"But why did he want to date me then?" Lindy frowned.

"I can't say for sure, but I've got an idea."

"You know," Lindy leaned over closer to Betty again, "I wondered why he never wanted to go to bed with me before that night. But why me? What did he want?"

"Lindy," Betty hesitated, "there was gossip. You see, talk gets around even in a city as large as Dallas. I heard a few years ago, about his father's will. In it his Daddy said if he didn't straighten out and marry before he was forty-five years old he would lose his inheritance. Everything would go to charities." Lindy sat speechless. "I can't say for sure, but I'd say he's going to be that on his birthday!"

"You mean that's why he's been dating me?"

"Honey, I'm sorry, but I can't imagine he has changed."

"I always wondered why he picked me when there are so many beautiful women here in Dallas. I was flattered that a rich handsome man wanted me."

"Lindy, you didn't know his history. Damn, I've got to get back to work. Will you be okay?" Betty stood up and stuffed the pack of cigarettes in her uniform pocket.

"I guess so," Lindy answered forlornly.

"Will I see you at Tony's tonight?"

"No, I've got the weekend off."

Betty leaned over, "Honey you rest and call me at home if you want to talk." Taking a napkin, she wrote down her telephone number. After Betty went back to work, Lindy sat dazed by what she'd learned. She felt humiliated and used: sickened over making love to a homosexual. He'd only wanted a marriage certificate.

I wonder what he'd planned to do with me after that, Lindy thought with a huff. First she'd met a con man that wanted her for her insurance money, and now a gay one, who needed her to save his inheritance. The future looked awfully bleak.

And what had she been thinking. She couldn't go to the police, certainly by now they were looking for her!

As Lindy shifted in the booth, the edge of the diamond ring in her jean pocket caught against her hip. She put her hand down and felt the outline of it.

Was it that bad witch again at work that caused a little smile to curl at the corner of her lips?

She left the coffee shop, hailed a taxi for downtown. In front of a jewelry store she asked the driver to wait for her.

"I wonder if you could check my ring for me, I think the stone is loose." She smiled at the friendly jeweler, as she took it off her hand.

"My goodness, you sure wouldn't want to lose this. Just give me a minute." He put on his glasses and sat at his worktable. His light sparkled on the stone and the platinum band. "There now Miss, its fine." He smiled at her and handed it back. "It's a beauty."

"Isn't it though? We're getting married next week and I sure wouldn't want anything to happen to it."

"It's in perfect shape."

"You know," Lindy smiled again, "I told my boyfriend not to spend a lot of money on a ring, but I'm sure he did."

"Well, I'd say you're a lucky girl."

"Tell me, just between us, what would he have paid? I promise not to tell

"Oh, I'd say around fifty thousand dollars." Lindy gasped.

"I knew it! I should have gone along with him. Lord, it's going to take us years to pay for this."

"Well, I say your boyfriend has good taste. No charge, just bring him in when you're in the market for something else."

"Oh, we'll be back." Lindy went out and stepped into the taxi and headed back to her motel room. She took the diamond ring off her finger. Felt the weight and the smoothness. Fifty thousand dollars! She had to think.

Could she marry Dade and live this lie? She'd have money and security. She could go to him and tell him she knew he was gay, and that he only wanted to marry her to keep his money. Maybe that would work! She put the ring back on her left hand, wiggled her fingers in the sunlight. Wow, it was beautiful! And she could have more, she was sure. What could he do after all? If what Betty had told her was true, he didn't have much time to find another bride.

Lindy yawned. It was early afternoon, and the effect of being up all night, and Dade's cruelty caught up with her. She crawled into bed and fell into a much needed sleep. She slept through the day, and awoke at midnight feeling rested. As if I would go along with Dade's twisted idea, she mumbled. No way!

Well, Dade Lampart, this just cost you!

Then remembering that it had been over a week since she'd placed that ad in the Dallas newspaper, she needed to check her post office box too. Maybe she would be rich again.

***

"Where to Miss?" the taxi driver asked as he carried Lindy's suitcases and put them in the trunk. Dade's big maroon Lexus stood just as she'd left it outside her motel room door. The driver's eyes grew large as he heard a series of banging, and turned in surprise just as the shattered glass from the windshield of the car fell to the ground. Then was silent as Lindy nonchalantly tossed a rock into the pile and got into the taxi. She didn't look back at the motel she'd called home, or Tony's where it had all started.

"Where to?" the cab driver asked again.

"The Regency Hotel, in downtown Dallas."

-20-

Reed sat at the bar in Flower Mound, Texas, martini in hand, not realizing how close he was to Lindy Lewis, and, pissed at the jerk's actions at Mitzi Grover's house. Would he give Mitzi the message to call? If he didn't hear by tomorrow, he'd personally go back and pound the shit out of the arrogant bastard. "How do the Cowboys look this year?" he turned to the bartender.

The lights in the bar were low as Tammy Wynette sang again about lost love. The door to the kitchen swung open and a waitress flew by balancing a tray of steaks and disappeared into the dining room. The rich, grilled aroma of prime meat lingered in the air, tantalizing Reed's stomach. The bartender smiled and replied, "They'll beat the hell out of that Wisconsin team."

"You're the one wanting a table?" The manager said just then with a harried look on his face. Reed followed him into the dining room. "Sorry about the wait. My hostess is off this weekend." He laid a menu on the table.

Betty came over with a big smile on her face and said, "Hello handsome. Good to see you again."

"How you doing?" Reed sat hunched over the table, drink in hand.

"I'm fine and busy as hell. How was your first night in our town?"

"Hm--, interesting." Reed answered raising an eyebrow. "Betty, I need a steak with all the trimmings."

"I can see you need some TLC. I'll bring you a salad and some bread so you won't waste away." She winked at him and swung her hips suggestively as she walked away. After wolfing down his dinner, Reed went back to the bar. He was still there a few hours later, when Betty slid up on the stool next to him. She had changed into a form fitting beige jumpsuit with a leopard belt. She'd let her hair down from the twist she'd worn earlier, and it curled around her face. Reed glanced up in surprise.

"Okay handsome, here's your chance to buy me a drink." She smiled up at him. "The manager let our hostess have the weekend off, and he doesn't know shit about the business."

"I can see it can get pretty hairy." Reed lit a cigarette.

Betty rolled her eyes and tasted her drink. "Hmm-- this tastes divine! How long are you going to be in town Reed?"

"Well, I don't know for sure, it all depends on how business goes."

"What kind of work do you do?" Betty asked as she openly studied his face.

"I'm in the insurance business. Pretty boring."

"Well, I guess it depends if you're buying or collecting." Betty reached into her purse for a package of cigarettes.

Wanting to change the subject, Reed asked, "How are your boys?" They sat together comfortably, as Betty talked about her family and the problems of being a single mother. Elvis sang to the crowded bar as the clock ticked close to midnight.

"Well Betty. I've got to go. Got an early appointment in the morning." Reed stood up and signed his charge card bill.

"Why don't you come over to my house for a drink? The boys are in bed. We can listen to music." Betty turned towards him as he prepared to leave.

"Gee thanks Betty. We'll have to make it another time, but I'll see you soon."

Reed left Tony's and went to his motel and sank into a deep sleep. In the morning, he waited to hear from Mitzi, but by afternoon she still hadn't called. He called her number and a machine urged him to leave a message. Steamed, he left his name and the number of the motel again with the hope that maybe this time she'd get the message. Reed spent the rest of the day and evening sitting around the motel room watching television. Totally bored. Mitzi didn't call. The next day, he went back to her apartment.

"What the hell, you again?" The same man peered through the crack in the doorways.

"Look, what's the deal here?" Reed's voice cracked. The man slammed the door, but not before Reed got his foot inside and pushed it open. Stepping into the foyer, he grabbed the man's shirt. Inches from his face Reed said, "Now, where's Mitzi?"

"She's not here. You can't push your way in here -- get out!"

Reed shoved him aside and walked in. "Watch me!" Reed bellowed back and charged through the house. He didn't say a word to the guy as he went out and slammed the door. After getting in his car, he drove around the block, came back and parked down the street. Sure enough, the guy came out and sped away. Reed slammed his fist on the steering wheel, muttered asshole and followed him. Then later he walked into the Flower Mound police department.

"I'm Reed Conners out of Minneapolis, Minnesota. I'm an investigator and I'd like to speak to one of your detectives about a missing person."

"You'd want to see Manny down the hall then." Reed walked into a cubicle that was small and airless like those found in police departments all over the country. Manny, a small wiry man with long hair and a drooping mustache looked up from a mountain of files.

"Manny, I'm told you're the man I want to see," Reed said and held out his hand.

After an hour, he left with an APB out for Lindy and her black BMW. State wide. He went back and watched Mitzi's apartment. It had been two days since he'd first tried to contact her. Finally, tired and depressed, Reed gave it up for the night and went back to his motel. He spent the first few days of the next week waiting for something to break. Nothing further developed.

Where the hell were they? Reed muttered. Later in the week he sat at Tony's Steakhouse and listened to the velvet voice of Elvis as he sang Born to Lose. A news flash came over the TV about a huge blizzard in the north, hundreds of accidents and damage to countless buildings because of the weight of the snow. Hard to imagine that going on while in the south it was eighty-six degrees and sunny.

The manager and bartender stood at the end of the bar talking in low tones. Suddenly, Reed's hand stopped in mid-air. Whiskey spilled over the edge of his glass and splashed on the bar. He turned to the men just after hearing, "Goddamn, Jack at the motel said Lindy's left and the room is cleaned out. Didn't even pay her bill!"

The bartender busily wiped glasses. "Maybe she's sick."

"Nah, I've seen her kind before. Comes in and works for awhile and then splits. I paid her in cash too."

A tingle of apprehension shot through Reed. Could they be talking about Lindy Lewis? Could she be here right under his nose? Betty slid up on a stool next to Reed.

"Hello handsome." She smiled at Reed and fussed with her hair.

"Betty, you're done work early tonight. Want your usual?"

"Lord, I need it." Betty lit a cigarette.

"Tough night?" Reed slid his stool around and faced her.

"It's been a busy week. I've had to both hostess and waitress."

"I just overheard the manager and bartender talking about the hostess quitting."

"Yeah, poor kid. After what she went through, I don't blame her for taking off." Betty chewed her bottom lip in thought.

"Her name was Lindy?" Reed asked carefully.

"Lindy Lewis," Betty replied and straightened her uniform skirt unaware of Reed's face as his eyes widened.

Be cool, he warned himself and asked, "She disappeared?"

"She never came back after her weekend off." Betty sipped her wine. "You know, she came in here a few months ago, broke and needing work. The boss put her up in the motel next door and gave her a job."

"Well, what happened? Sounds like she had it made." Reed lifted his glass carefully and drank. Intent and anxious.

"Well, she seemed to be getting on her feet, but then she met up with that ass-hole standing right over there." Betty nodded her head towards a man standing at the bar on the other side of the room.

Reed glanced over. Suddenly possessiveness gripped his stomach. Steeling himself to stay calm, he asked, "Where was Lindy Lewis from?"

"Somewhere way up north, I guess. That's right; she mentioned Minnesota's weather one time."

Reed's heart picked up a beat as he asked, "Would you like another glass of wine Betty? It's still early."

"Gosh, I shouldn't."

"Oh, come on Betty. Live a little."   She looked at him in surprise.

"Okay, just one then."   They sat and drank in silence for a few minutes. Reed didn't want to rush her, but he thought she might have a lot more to say. He kept an eye on the guy across the bar.

"Betty, who is that man?"   He finally had to ask and Betty laughed.

"A bad ass from way back and he's as queer as a three dollar bill!"

"What?"   Reed looked at him openly now. Betty hiccupped, then covered her mouth with a hand. "Betty, if he's gay, what did he want with Lindy?"

Betty whispered, "He ran a game on her. Then raped her!"   Reed gulped, tried to steady himself.

"Jesus, he raped her, what's his name?"

"Dade Lampart. He has quite a reputation around town. Rich too."

"The son of a bitch!" Reed's knuckles were white as he gripped the glass of liquor he was holding. "Did she go to the police? The hospital?"

Betty shook her head. "She wouldn't! I tried to convince her to, but she said she was okay."

"What's his angle?"

Betty shrugged. "From what I heard, the guy needs to get married before the end of the year or else he loses his millions. Daddy's will."

Reed leaned in closer, missing nothing. "So he was romancing Lindy Lewis to marry her?"

"Yes, I'd say so. She didn't know anything about him until I told her."

"Lindy Lewis was broke huh," Reed asked then?

"Not a dime I guess. I know the boss gave her a few bucks in advance to live on when she first started." Betty moved in closer to Reed. "You know, I'm tired of talking about the hostess. Why don't you come over to my house?"

"God, I'm sorry Betty. I've got a lot of paper work to do tonight before a meeting in the morning. Insurance you know."

"Well, maybe another time." Betty slid off her stool. Reed kissed her on the cheek as she turned to leave. "Sure you can't make it?" She winked at him.

"Yeah, but I'll see you soon." He looked over the bar at Dade Lampart. Their eyes met for just a second, and a thread of curiosity flashed across the space. Reed ordered another drink and sat hunched over the bar as his mind worked furiously. Lindy Lewis was here in Dallas. Or had been. If she was broke, what the hell had happened to the million dollars? She'd worked for two months, played around with this guy and been raped by him. Now she'd disappeared again.

Reed glanced over at Dade Lampart again with ambivalent feelings. He took a swallow of his drink. Be cool, he warned himself again, but his fingers itched to put them around this ass hole's neck and wring the truth out of him. Make him squirm.

The next day, Reed checked in with Manny at the police department. "Nothing yet on that dame and her car, Reed. I'd say she's left town."

"Maybe--, maybe not." Reed sat across the desk from his new acquaintance. "You got any coffee?"

"Just made some. Black?" Manny asked and handed Reed a steaming cup.

"Manny, what do you know about a guy named Dade Lampart?"

"You kidding me? He's a local. Rich and queer." Manny laughed.

"What's his agenda?" Reed got up out of his chair and began to pace.

"I heard he inherited millions from his old man." Manny looked at Reed. "You got something? I wouldn't mind helping you out, my friend. Fucking queer!"

"I don't know yet Manny. I'll let you know." Reed left after agreeing to stay in touch. He drove out to Lampart's ranch.

This guy got lucky, Reed muttered when he saw the place from a safe distance. The mansion sat on a hill, and overlooked cattle and horses grazing in the fenced pastures. Ranch hands worked in the yards. Reed waited and watched Lampart's place and later Mitzi's apartment.

"Oh hell," Reed swore disgustedly as he sat in his motel after a week. He threw his clothes on a chair and went to bed. The air-conditioner hummed against the hot humid night common in Texas this time of the year. He slept fitfully and awakened early. He was going back out to Lampart's ranch to look around.

Showered and dressed in jeans and a tee shirt, he opened the motel door and stepped out into blazing sunshine. He squinted against the glare as he walked to his car. Then blinked and looked again.

His eyes widened and he ran across the parking lot and stopped dead in his tracks. All the windows in his Corvette were smashed. The tires flat. Glass cracked under his boots as he walked closer. He leaned inside and the glass covered the entire surface of the seats and floor. He looked around the area warily. It was a typical neighborhood of old homes, warehouses and small businesses. About a half mile away, the sign from Tony's Steakhouse towered above the trees. He unlocked the glove compartment and saw his CD's were still there.

"Must have gotten scared off before they could get these," he muttered under his breath. Pissed as hell, he went back to his room and called the police and his insurance company.

"It'll be ready in three days," the mechanic said. Do you need a loaner?"

"Do you have a black sedan?" Reed answered. The nerve of someone touching his property.

The next few days, Reed followed Mitzi's boyfriend and watched Dade Lampart's ranch. He found out that her boyfriend fooled around with other women and peddled drugs and Lampart hired illegals from across the border. He stopped at Tony's for dinner and later Betty joined him at the bar.

"I can't imagine where she'd go, poor kid," she said in answer to Reed's question as to whether she'd heard from Lindy Lewis.

"Well, I think I'll have to leave soon and get back to my home office." Reed turned to face her. "Sorry, we couldn't get together, who knows--." He raised his hand in question and winked at her.

"Oh, all the good ones leave." Betty smiled sadly as she slid off the stool and picked up her purse. "Stop in at the coffee shop one day and I'll buy you breakfast."

"Sure, thanks Betty. Sleep fast, morning comes early."

"Tell me about it," she said with a tired smile.

Reed had been in Texas three weeks, and Lindy's trail had grown cold. Frustration deepened the lines on his face as he went back to his motel room. He was pissed and restless. His gut told him Lindy had left Dallas and he was wasting his time staying around. Manny would notify him if the APB brought her in. Damn, he'd hit the road early in the morning; get back to Minnesota and relax and wait for the ice to freeze on his lake so he could fish.

He unlocked the door to his motel room, stepped in and immediately sensed something was wrong! Chills vibrated up his spine as he stood still, silhouetted in the doorway. Moonlight filtered into the room through the thin shades and as his eyes adjusted to the gloomy interior, he saw his clothes had been torn off hangers and laying on the floor. Dresser drawers were open and his underwear strewn about.

"What--?" was all Reed Conners could say before the world exploded and a million stars crashed through his head. He lay on the floor with his arms twisted under his body. The clock on the bedside table ticked quietly as the traffic roared on the busy street just outside but nothing moved inside the motel room for several stunned minutes. Then Reed opened his eyes, gasped for air as dust from the carpet tickled his nose. He tried to move. But the pain! He dropped his head back to the floor. His breath, harsh and labored. He needed to get his gun. Moving slowly and steeling himself for another blow in the dark room, he reached for his holster.

Christ, his gun was gone! He lay still, a pigeon, unable to defend himself. Minutes went by.

Goddamn, he thought fiercely to himself, if someone is waiting for another shot at me, here's their chance to take me out.

Reed jumped up suddenly and whirled around the room. All was quiet. He stood on shaky legs, then felt the burning sensation in his shoulder. When his hand came away covered in blood, he sagged down on the bed, weak and dazed.

Christ, someone had tried to kill him! And just before he passed out, a thought skittered across his mind. Was Lindy involved in this?

-21-

The man in the orange prison suit jumped up and took a deep drag on his cigarette. Sweat poured down his forehead as he stood in the recreation room at the Kansas prison. It was late fall. The weather hot and humid. His contacts had finally come through with what he needed to know. Reed Conners was in Dallas, Texas and wherever he was, Lindy Lewis would be close by. Time was of the essence. John Thomas had patiently waited and now everything was in place, just waiting to be put into action.

***

"Umm, that feels good," Lindy said to the masseuse' as she used her practiced hands on Lindy's back. The sheet draped over her lower back slid further down as the therapist massaged and soothed. Relaxing music played on the stereo. As Lindy lay on the table she let her thoughts ramble. She'd been at the Regency Hotel in downtown Dallas for over a week, established on the nineteenth floor, which overlooked the city. The view was breathtaking, especially at night. As yet, she'd not received any response from her ad in the Dallas newspaper offering a ten thousand dollar reward for information on the whereabouts of her BMW that was stolen from her, so she'd decided to run it two more weeks. Sooner or later, she was sure she'd find the culprit who had her car and money. It had taken time to find a pawnshop that would give her the money she knew Dade's engagement ring was worth, but she'd found one and now she had fifty thousand dollars in the hotel safe. Enough money to tide her over until she found her million dollars. Today, she had an appointment at Niemen-Marcus for a makeover. She needed a new look!

"This is it" she said excitedly to the girl at the department store's beauty center. "I love it!"

"Are you sure?"

"Absolutely!" Lindy's eyes gleamed as she checked herself in a mirror.

"Can I put you down for another appointment?" The beauty consultant wrote Lorna Lee on the appointment book and smiled at her customer's pleasure. Now, Lindy had the look she wanted; blonde hair to go with the brown contacts she bought to cover her blue eyes. Her new identity.

She called for a reservation in the hotel dining room downstairs. Her Mother's diamond and ruby earrings sparkled on her ears as she stepped out of the elevator. Heads turned as she walked into the restaurant.

"Good evening, Miss Lee," the Matre' D greeted her. "I have your usual table. Say, I like your look. I wouldn't have recognized you on the street."

"Does it look good Andre'?"

"Knocks my socks off!" The gray-haired man chuckled and smiled appreciatively as he eyed her up and down, then led her to a table. Lindy was unaware she was whispered about as 'that mysterious gal' in the penthouse.

That night she awoke out of a sound sleep. It was three o'clock in the morning and as she lay in her luxurious surroundings, she willed herself to relax. Her body hurt and her arms and legs trembled. She shivered under the covers, and after lying awake for hours got up and paced around her hotel room.

"It must have been a bug I picked up," she told Andre' as she came into the dining room the next day for lunch.

"Well, I thought you were looking a little peaked lately, but you look great now." Lindy smiled at his compliments as he pulled out her chair and waited for her to be seated.

After lunch, she went to a movie, lingered over a light dinner and then went back to her room where she kicked off her shoes, undressed and slipped into a cozy robe. Lindy planned a quiet evening, but as she bent her head down to tie the belt when she straightened up, a sudden pain shot through her head. Startled, Lindy caught her breath and her eyes widened in surprise. She walked over to the window, taking small careful steps. Her hand went to her head and her heart began to speed out of control. Then, as suddenly as the pain had appeared, it went away. Dismissing the sudden strangeness, Lindy sat down on the couch, pulled her robe tightly around herself and turned on the television. Later that night, she again awakened from a sound sleep. This time panic enveloped her as the events of the past year coursed through her thoughts. Flames from her house fire smothered her. Remembering again J.T.'s death chase on the highway and Dade Lampart squeezing the breath out of her as he held her down.

Awakening terrified, she huddled for warmth as she fought a need to run and hide. She got up and began pacing again. She walked until she was exhausted and finally she slept. The next day she felt fine.

"Good morning, Miss Lee," Andre' the Matre' D greeted her as she came into the Regency dining room late in the morning. "You look like you need a cup of coffee right away. Were you out late last night?"

"Something like that." Lindy gave him a weak smile and waited anxiously for him to return.

"Are you all right?" he asked again.

"I just need some food I think." Lindy ordered breakfast, but as she lifted the cup of coffee to her lips for the last few drops; something strange happened. Her mind went blank, absolutely numbing her sense of familiarity. She sat frozen as her hand held the cup suspended in mid-air and as she lowered it, it clattered against the saucer. She ran her hands over her arms as a chill spread, then clasped them over her chest as she sat dumbfounded, amongst the busy chatter of the dining room.

Terror began in small trickles, then inched through her. A large sign on the wall said Regency. But where? She looked down at her hands; slim fingers, long painted nails. They belonged to a stranger. She didn't know herself, couldn't feel the comfort of her own warmth. For a moment she wondered; was she dying and this the in-between?

A key with the number, 1902 lay on the table beside a black purse.

"Thanks, Lorna. You have a good day," a waiter said as he placed a tray with change down on the table. It came as another shock, when she realized she hadn't known her name.

"Will we see you for dinner, Miss Lee?" Andre' asked as she walked out of the room on shaky legs. She forced a weak smile on her face, but couldn't answer. Her breath came out in short little gasps as she walked through the lobby of the hotel.

What had happened to her? What should she do?

She clutched the hotel key in her hand and hurried to the refuge of the room, but as she stepped out of the elevator on the nineteenth floor and cautiously opened the door to 1902, she steeled herself for what she might find.

Was there someone in there waiting for her?

She took a few faltering steps into the silent room and then collapsed in the nearest chair. Her purse dropped to the floor and the contents spilled out. She looked around the room that she'd spent over a week in, seeing it for the first time. Nothing looked familiar. She glanced into a mirror and a stranger stared back at her. Panic gripped her as she sat immobilized, unable to think. Unaware of time, maybe hours later, she got up and walked into the bedroom of her suite. The room was decorated in peach and cream. She opened the closet door and ran her hand over the clothes. She opened the dresser drawers and felt the delicate underwear.

Were these her things? Now her body began to tremble uncontrollably. She sat on the bed and clasped the satin bed cover for comfort. It felt cold and stiff. Just a hint of perfume hung in the air.

Oh God help me! She cried, then dialed 911.

Within thirty minutes, Lindy sat in the emergency room of the Dallas Memorial Hospital. Curtains partitioned off the cubicle, but didn't shut out the sounds of people in pain, or the antiseptic odors. A kind-faced nurse came in with a clipboard.

"Your name, please?"

"Lorna Lee," Lindy replied, pale and shaken. "That's what they called me at the hotel."

"Take your time," the nurse said and put her hand on Lindy's arm reassuringly. "Can you tell me what happened, Miss Lee?"

"I don't know!" Lindy got off the examining table, her eyes on the door.

"Miss Lee, it's okay, we'll help you! Now just sit down and take some deep breaths. Are you in pain?"

"No--," Lindy answered.

"Have you been having headaches?"

"No--, Yes." Lindy answered again. "I can't remember. I don't remember anything." She started to cry.

"Now Lorna, don't panic. Do you have some identification in your purse, in your billfold?"

Lindy wiped her eyes. Her hands shook as she opened her purse and took out a red leather billfold. She held it and turned it over, seeing it for the first time. The snap echoed in the small enclosure as she opened it. Then her eyes widened as she looked at a driver's license with a picture. She started to shake again, gasping for breath as she showed it to the nurse.

"Now its okay, I'll just get the doctor," the woman said and left hurriedly. The sound of her crepe-soled shoes swooshed on the tiled floor. Lindy sat in the curtained enclosure and stared at the picture of a brunette with blue eyes. A stranger named Lindy Lewis. Then at the Minnesota address!

Where was she now? Why did the people at the hotel call her Lorna Lee? Blackness swirled up from the floor to meet her. She looked up a few minutes later as a man in a white coat moved the curtain aside and stepped in.

"Miss Lee, I'm Doctor Horton. Well, my dear, let's have a look at you." He pulled up a chair and sat down beside her bed. His middle-aged face was kind, his voice soothing. "Can you tell me what happened?" Lindy sat up straighter now, but twisted the tissue in her hand.

"I don't know!" She tried to control her voice to stop the trembling in her body.

"It's okay. You're safe here. Miss Lee. Did you wake up feeling this way this morning?"

Lindy whispered, "I don't know!"

"We'll just check some things, Miss Lee." Lindy sat tensed as he poked, listened and shined his light. "Do you know where you were when you lost your memory?"

"I had a room key and it said the Regency Hotel in Dallas, Texas." Her face was ghostly white.

"You are in Dallas Miss Lee. What year is this?" No answer came from her lips. "Do you know who our president is?" Again, Lindy could only stare at him in silence. "I want to do some further tests, so I'll want you to stay here for awhile. Maybe a day or two." He moved towards the door. "Just try not to panic, we'll find out what's wrong." He smiled kindly at her as he opened the curtain. He motioned to the same nurse. "Stay with Miss Lee and get her settled."

"Okay honey don't worry now," she reassured Lindy. "That doctor is special and he'll fix you in no time," she said pushing in a wheelchair. The trip up the elevator and down the long halls in the hospital was a blur to Lindy. Finally, the nurse wheeled her into a room and smiled, "Now, I'll help you get undressed and into bed. I want you to rest, and then Doctor Horton will be back in to see you." She hung up Lindy's red silk dress and lined her black patent pumps against the wall in the closet. The nurse tied the strings on the gown and tucked Lindy into bed and then left.

The downtown lights of Dallas had come on spreading a soft glow over the stark room. Dinner carts rattled on the tile floor leaving a trail of tuna and noodles, cinnamon and coffee, as Lindy lay back on the hard pillow. Just as panic threatened to strangle her again, Doctor Horton's familiar face came into view. He put a hand on her shoulder, "Now Miss Lee, its okay. Take some deep breaths. I'm going to give you a shot so you can sleep tonight, but first I wonder if you can stand and walk for me."

Back in bed, Lindy felt a needle prick her arm and then the warm blanket of a drug crept through her body, dragging her tired eyelids down as she slid gratefully into the softness of sleep while the clanking, busy noise of the place receded into nothing.

The next day was a maze of tests with humming machines and Lindy began to relax after another night of sound sleep. She awoke as a nurse slid a table with breakfast in front of her. The aroma of bacon and toast tickled her nose. Just then, Doctor Horton came in. Lindy liked his gentle manner, crisp gray hair and kind eyes. He pulled a chair over to the bed and sat down. She looked at him anxiously as he paged through a chart.   "Well Miss Lee, all the tests came back negative. I was concerned about several things, but fortunately I was wrong."   Lindy waited for more. "Have you remembered anything?" When she shook her head, the doctor went on, "I've discussed your case with my colleagues and we've agreed you have what's called hysterical amnesia."

Fearfully, Lindy looked at him and pushed the breakfast table away from her bed; then swung her legs over the edge. With her painted toenails bright in the morning sunshine she looked at him helplessly and asked, "What is that?"

"Well--, it's caused by stress. Stressful and painful events. You see, sometimes, when our minds get so full of unpleasantness, we shut down. We can't accept any more. Most of the time, it's a temporary thing."

Lindy looked wide-eyed at the Doctor and said, "When the nurse and I looked at my driver's license, it said Lindy Lewis. And I'm from Minnesota!"

"I know. Let's take another look at that."
Lindy reached in her purse for the red billfold. She
handed it to the Doctor and slid further under the
covers. He studied the picture for a few minutes
then said, "Miss Lee, this is you! You're eyes are
really blue, you know. You had them covered with
brown contacts. And your hair has been lightened."
Bewildered, Lindy reached for the picture and
studied it again.

"You know, I can call the authorities. See if
there's a missing person report out for you.
Perhaps we'll find someone to come for you."

A tremor shot through Lindy's body.
Something didn't sound right about that. Doctor
Horton sensed her sudden fear and consoled her,
"Well, I want you to get another night of sleep and
we'll see tomorrow. I think when you're well
rested, things will right themselves." He smiled
reassuringly as he left.

Lindy slept the day away and again soundly
into that night. She awoke as someone said, "Miss
Lee, I just need to check your blood pressure." In
her drowsiness, Lindy wondered, "Why are you
calling me Miss Lee, its Lewis?" She opened her
eyes then. A frown crossed her face as she sat up.
She remembered everything! After the nurse left,
she threw the covers off and stood up. Everything
fit again. She knew who she was, and why she had
changed her identity!

But what if Doctor Horton had notified the police! She had to leave, get away fast! She found her clothes, dressed and ran a hand through her hair. She peeked out the door and not seeing anyone around, quickly found the stairs. She ended up in the same part of the hospital she'd come into, days ago. The Emergency Center. She called a taxi and stepped around a corner, to stay out of sight. Sirens screamed then as an ambulance approached the hospital. Curiously, Lindy stepped out of her hiding place just as paramedics brought a wounded man in on a stretcher.

"Gun shot!" they yelled to the medical staff running to meet them. In the seconds that followed before jumping back out of sight, Lindy recognized the man.

My God, she whispered, it's Reed Conners!

-22-

The September morning sunshine awakened Reed Conners as he lay in the Dallas hospital. The night had been a foggy blur of pain, but he knew instantly where he was and that someone had tried to kill him.

He raised his hand and felt the bandage that covered his right shoulder, the sling around his arm. His mouth tasted like a tin can. He winced as he tried to sit up to reach a glass of water on the bedside table, then fell back down on the pillow, pissed when the pain immobilized him.

"Where the hell is everybody?" he grumbled. The door opened and Betty stepped in.

"God, what are you doing here?" he muttered as she came over to his bed and kissed him on the cheek.

"Well, someone has to worry about you." She was still wearing her black work uniform.

She looked him over critically. "The doctor said you were lucky. If the gun-shot had been an inch lower, you'd been in real trouble."

A sheen of sweat broke out over Reed's face. He punched the coarse cotton blanket that covered him with his good hand.

"Here's some water," Betty held the glass to his lips as he drank. "Now you've got to rest so you can heal, Reed."

"Yeah," he said, depressed and hurting. The busy activity of the hospital hummed with squeaking carts, banging metal objects and constant paging on the intercom.

"Aren't you supposed to be at the coffee shop?" Reed asked then.

Betty sat down on a nearby chair. "I called in and took the day off."

Reed looked at her and realized it felt good to have a woman worrying about him. "How did you know I was here?"

Betty stood up and began to straighten the covers on his bed. "When I got home last night, I got to feeling blue. I just thought being it was your last night here--. Anyway, I called your motel room, and they said there had been an accident."

"You mean you've been here all night?"

"Well, I guess." Betty sat down again. Fine lines graced her face. "The doctor said you'll have to be here at least four days. That's providing there are no complications."

"Yeah?" Reed grumbled again. "Can you find some coffee in this goddamn place?"   Minutes later, she came back carrying a steaming cup and helped him as he grasped it in shaky hands.

"Thanks Betty," Reed said a few minutes later in a slightly better mood. "Go home now and get some sleep."

"You sure you're going to be okay? I called the boys and they're getting ready for school."

He put the cup of coffee down and gave her a weak smile. "I'll be okay."

After she left, with the caffeine clearing Reed's head; a faint memory slipped back. It had been plaguing him all night, but in his drugged mind he wondered if it had actually happened? His shoulder throbbed and burned. But, he'd be damned if he'd take any more drugs. He had to figure this out.

Somewhere, sometime during the night he had seen Lindy Lewis! But where, he had no idea!

Had she been the one who had shot him? Would she actually want to hurt him that much? The money she'd gotten illegally from burning down her house couldn't mean that much! But, then again, it had been years since he'd really been around her.

He clenched his teeth as he moved in the hospital bed. Would a million dollars be worth it? Then again, it could have been Lampart. He did employ illegals from across the border. But Mitzi's boy friend? Nah, he mumbled, he's small time. Reed exhaled in frustration and closed his eyes.

God the pain! Everything hurt!

The next few days lumbered by as Reed bitched continually about not being out there looking for the killer. Manny from the police department came in just as his breakfast arrived one morning.

"Buddy, I got your message, I've been in Houston. What the hell happened?" Manny's long hair was pulled back in a pony tail. His faded denim shirt matched the jeans he was wearing. The scent of his heavy cologne had preceded him as he came in the door.

Reed sat up, his face anxious as he said, "Christ, it's good to see you. I was blasted the minute I opened my motel door. My room had been ransacked."

"You didn't get a look at anyone?" Manny took out a book and started writing down notes.

"Man, I didn't get a chance! They got my gun too." Reed pushed his tray of food out of the way. "God awful stuff, they pass off as nourishing."

"Think man," Manny said.

Grudgingly, Reed replied, "When I stepped in, I saw my room had been ripped apart. The next thing I knew, I was laying on the floor. Shot!"

"Why did you say they? Do you think it was more than one person?" Manny's dark eyes were intense.

"Christ, I don't know," Reed pulled the sling off his arm and moved his shoulder. "I didn't see anyone. This still hurts like hell," he muttered.

Manny snapped his notebook shut and pulled up a chair. "Anything new on Lindy Lewis yet? We've got nothing on the APB we've had out on her."

"Not a clue! I lost her after she left the job at Tony's Steakhouse."   Reed adjusted his two hundred pound frame in the small bed and the plastic covered mattress squeaked as he moved. His sandy hair fell over his face.

"Manny," he said thoughtfully, "at first I thought I had imagined this, but I saw her somewhere, the night they brought me in here!" Reed swung his bare legs over the edge of the bed and stood up.

"Manny," he said again, "I need you to check out something for me, if you will." Reed walked around his room slowly and shook his head. "I know it was her!"

He got back in his bed and exhaled loudly. "At first I thought it was the drugs that had screwed me up. When I came in I was fading in and out. I remember the bumpy ride and then the presence of people moving around--yelling. Then suddenly they shot me full of drugs!"

"When did you see her?"

Reed's face paled from the exertion and he lay back on the pillow. "Just before I passed out for good, I looked up and there she stood."

"Are you sure?"

"Manny, I know for sure. Have you got some time?"

"Yeah, you've got me intrigued now." Manny ran his fingers through his mustache.

"Okay thanks," Reed exhaled. "Get her picture and check to see if she was visiting someone here, or a patient maybe. She's blonde now."

"I'll contact the taxi companies to see who's been driving her around. Maybe get an address."

Reed closed his eyes and tried to sleep after Manny left. Why the hell had this happened just when he'd decided to go back home? To the peace and quiet of the north.

Christ, would this mess ever be cleaned up? John Thomas was in jail, but only after he'd killed Tanner Burke and Tanner's girl friend, Sierra Ames. And if he had found Lindy in Dallas and got the million back, the case would be closed, finally!

When Reed awoke later, Betty was sitting by his bed. He sat up and pulled the covers up over his bare legs. "When did you get here?" he asked.

"Just now," she smiled coyly. She was beginning to look better all the time to him.

"You don't need to come so often Betty, I know you're busy with two jobs and the boys."

"I don't mind Reed. Listen, I talked to the doctor and you can leave tomorrow, but only if you have someone to stay with you. And since you don't, you can stay with us for awhile."

"Oh Betty, I don't know." He had a feeling about this, but he had to get out of here.

"Reed, it'll be just a few days," Betty urged.

Realizing he didn't have a choice, he said, "Okay, thanks Betty. I'll try not to be a nuisance."

Later, the next day he was enthroned on the couch in Betty's den. He had to admit it felt rather good to have her fuss over him. He picked up the phone Betty had put near his bed.

"Manny, I'm out. Here's where I'll be for awhile. Have you found anything?"

"Yup, been waiting to hear from you. Get this: Lindy Lewis was a patient in the Dallas Hospital for three days. Looks like you ran into her just as she was leaving."

"What the hell was going on?" Reed sat up.

"I had to pull some strings," Manny said. "She was diagnosed as having something called hysterical amnesia. Lost her memory. Didn't know who the hell she was! The Doctor said its from stress--too much for the mind to handle."

"I'll be damned, will her memory come back?"

"Apparently it all came back and she split in the middle of the night."

"What else?" Reed asked, but guiltily felt an immediate sense of relief.

"Oh yeah, she's going by the name of Lorna Lee. There's more but I'm leaving this for you. She's holed up in that fancy Regency Hotel in downtown Dallas!"

Reed stood up then. On the way to the closet for his coat, he said into the telephone, "Buddy, I owe you one." His steps were slower, but determined as he left Betty's house.

"Lindy Lewis," he muttered as the Corvette roared into action out on the freeway, "I'm going to get you yet!"

-23-

L indy gaped at the wounded man on the stretcher. She stepped back and clamped a hand over her mouth as he was pushed down the hallway and into an enclosed area. Her taxi had stopped outside the hospital door. Its blinking light reflected in the glass window. She hesitated for a second, then ran out the door, the night air, damp on her flushed face. "Regency Hotel," she whispered to the driver.

Reed Conners had found her, but my God, he'd been shot they'd said!

She remembered the blood. What if he died, she thought and sat up abruptly. She'd have the taxi driver turn around and go back to the hospital. Oh--, I've got to think, she whimpered, then hurried through the lobby at the hotel and into her room. Unable to sleep any more that night she paced the floor until the first light of day, then picked up the telephone.

"Dallas Memorial Hospital," a voice greeted her.

"Can you tell me how Reed Conners is today?" She took a deep breath as she nervously waited, then thought my God is he still alive?

"Are you family?" the voice asked Lindy.

"Yes, someone called me. I'm his sister, I'm calling from North Dakota." As the small fib rolled off her lips Lindy sat on her bed, hoping the person couldn't tell she was in the same city

"Well, in that case I guess its okay to tell you-- Mr. Conners is in serious condition. That's all I can tell you, you'll have to talk to his Doctor."

"Thank you, I'll call him."   Lindy lay back in the king-sized bed, relieved but sick at heart.

"Well, Lindy Lewis, what are you going to do now?" she asked herself.

Apparently Reed had found her, but who had shot him? And why?

Should she go to him? She wondered what he would say if she told him the million dollars was gone? She grimaced then and realized she needed to check the post office again. Just maybe the thief had seen her ad in the paper.

She showered and dressed and the taxi she called was there in five minutes. When she opened the post office box with her key she gasped in surprise. A plain white envelope lay there. Her hand shook as she reached in for it. Just the post office box number was typed on the front. Lindy ripped it open. It read; Russell's Bar and Diner October 4th- 9:00 P.M. Wear red. Bring money.

My God! Could it mean she'd get her car and the money back after all these months? The date was two days away.

She paced around her room again. Could this be a set-up? But, she'd know her BMW anywhere and she had to take a chance.

October fourth finally arrived. Lindy went to her deposit box in the hotel and counted out some of the cash she had saved from Dade's ring as her taxi waited. She jammed the letter in her purse and ran back out to the taxi.

"Just let this go right," she whispered looking at her watch. It was eight forty-five. She'd dressed in a red blouse. Her knees shook as she opened the door of the bar and walked in. Cigarette smoke and stale beer greeted her. The place was so dark it took her a minute to get accustomed to the gloom. She stumbled against someone's foot as she made a quick beeline to an empty booth. She put her purse and the canvas bag containing the money down on the seat beside her and looked around cautiously. It was a workingman's bar located in the warehouse part of town. The customers wore work boots and dusty jeans. Couples swayed to the music of Roy Orbison. A waitress came by carrying a tray of burgers and fries and Lindy's stomach did a flip-flop over the smell of grease left in the wake.

Would she recognize the man? She jumped when the waitress asked, "What'll you have honey?"

She had to order something. "A brandy Manhattan," Lindy said, her voice coming out in a whisper.

"Can't hear you honey," the waitress said loudly over the music.

"A brandy Manhattan," Lindy replied again. It didn't appeal to her, but maybe it would settle her stomach. Right now, she had to take small breaths to still the nausea that threatened to well up in her throat. She lit a cigarette. It tasted awful.

"Sorry, I didn't mean to rush you; it's just that we're short of help tonight." The waitress put Lindy's drink down on the table.

Lindy took a quick drink before she answered, "That's okay; I'm not in any rush."

"I haven't seen you in here before, are you new in town?" The girl had dark hair and a friendly smile.

"Yes, just got here," Lindy said, "Do you know of any jobs? I'm a waitress too."

"Really, we need help here. Talk to Arnie!"

"Well, not now, but I'll be back later." Lindy answered. She noticed from her nametag that her name was Jenny. Lindy needed her.

"Okay," Jenny continued, "the tips are good, but some of the customers are pigs! You know what I mean."

"I sure do, they're the same all over." Lindy gave Jenny a conspiratorial look.

"We'd have fun working together though." Jenny rolled her eyes as customers banged their empty glasses on the next table. Lindy took another sip of the drink and looked at her watch. It was nine o'clock right on the dot. Her heart thumped in her chest as Vince Gill's voice came on the jukebox. Lights dimmed as couples scrambled to the dance floor to sway to the slow, romantic music. The air was damp with humidity as the ceiling fans worked overtime. Lindy willed her nerves to be still. Just then a man slid into the seat across from her. She looked up into his eyes.

"Where's the money?" he asked in a gruff voice. He was young; somewhere in his twenties. A baseball cap covered his hair. Dark glasses hid his eyes and a full mustache decorated his pockmarked dark face.

"Where's my car?" Lindy asked.

"In the lot across the street!" He drummed his fingers on the table and asked again, "Where is it?"

Lindy raised the canvas bag and opened it just enough for him to see the neatly stacked bills bundled together. She motioned for Jenny, the waitress, to come over. "We're going outside to check on something, could you put my bag somewhere safe for me? Just make-up and things."

"Oh sure, I'll put it in my locker with my purse, it'll be fine." Jenny took the bag to the back, not realizing what she was carrying. The man's face reddened as he watched the waitress walk away.

Lindy stood up and said, "Now, I want to see my car. You didn't wreck it did you?" He mumbled "Oh fuck!" They walked out together and to anyone who might have been watching, they looked like an average couple going out to get some air. They rounded a corner and in amongst the rows of cars stood a black BMW. Lindy's heart lurched. The license plate was hers. Her breath came out in little short puffs as she said, "Open it; I want to check the inside!"

"For Christ's sake lady! It's yours! I don't have time for this."

"You don't think I'm going to give you thousands of dollars until I'm sure it's mine and everything is still in it, do you?" Asshole! She was terrified but needed to put up a fearless front.

"Okay, okay!" He opened the door with his set of keys. "Check it out, I put a few miles on it, but that's all."   He stepped back and pulled his cap lower on his forehead.

"Well, I don't believe you. Let me see!" Lindy said as she slid into the seat.

"You'd better not try anything funny!" He put a hand inside his jacket pocket. Lindy's heart lurched in her chest as she closed the car door. The inside looked the same. The same air freshener was still hanging on the mirror. Her lipstick and change laying in the console. Her eyes flew to the passenger's seat and in a swift action with her wrist, ripped open a corner of the back rest. There it was! Stacks of money, just as she'd hidden it months ago.

Be calm, she warned herself, you can't let him see anything. She whipped the upholstery back, and turned in the seat and scanned the back, just to make her search look believable. She got out of the car and slammed the door.

"You didn't take my spare tires did you? I want to see the trunk!"

The man was sweating and yelled, "Lady, you got your fucking car. I don't have all night!"

"Well, I do!"   Lindy bluffed. "Okay, I'm satisfied," Lindy finally said and they went back inside the bar.

"I'll take my bag when you have a minute," Lindy said to Jenny as they stood at the bar. Her underarms were drenched. When Jenny returned with the bag, Lindy handed it to the man and said, "It's all there, you can go in the men's room and count it if you want. I'll wait here for the keys!" This was it!

The man looked uncertain, then turned and hurried off. The second he disappeared, Lindy took off through the door and raced to her car, the extra set of keys in her hand. She looked frantically over her shoulder as she fled and fumbled with the lock, but finally got the door open and climbed in just as a voice yelled an obscenity. In seconds she was out of the parking lot.

"Asshole, you got a hundred bucks!" She sped off, half expecting gun shots.

The Texas skies lit up as lightening cracked across the darkness. Raindrops danced in the dust. She hit the freeway, and drove on and off the exits, making sure she wasn't being followed. When she finally realized she was alone; she relaxed and gave an ear-shattering shriek. Her hands shook on the steering wheel. Her heart thumped; but she had her money. It had been one chance in a million, but she had hit the jackpot.

Back at her hotel, she threw her clothes in suitcases and flew down the back stairs. In less than an hour, she was on the road again in her BMW. She was on her way to an island on the southeast coast that beckoned. The first thing she was going to do was rent a safe deposit box, then call up her old friend Mitzi Grover back in Dallas. She had enough money now to treat both herself and Mitzi to a well deserved vacation.

-24-

"Goddamn Lindy," Reed cussed and shifted gears as pain radiated down through his arm from the gun-shot wound in his shoulder. "You've jerked me around long enough!" The streets flew by leading to the freeway as he headed to the Regency Hotel where she'd been traced and hiding out under the name of Lorna Lee.

The Texas skies were a vibrant blue and the traffic; bumper to bumper. Sweat ran down Reed's forehead as he punched the gas pedal on the Corvette.

Where the hell was everyone going? These people are nuts rushing around like this, he mumbled as his hands clenched the wheel. The hotel was right in the middle of downtown Dallas; settled in amongst the tall buildings on Tenth and Broadway. He got out of the heavy traffic, found a parking spot and crossed a street to the tall granite structure; many stories high. Uniformed doormen stood outside opening car doors, greeting customers and blowing whistles for Taxis. Reed ignored the men and walked right up to the check-in counter. Not wasting time, he said to the front desk clerk, "I need Lorna Lee's room number!"

"Excuse me sir?" A young man said raising an eyebrow.

Already pissed at the clerk's attitude, Reed tried again. "What room is Lorna Lee in?"

"We don't give out that information. Sorry." The desk clerk stepped back with a dismissing air.

"Pardon me," Reed said patiently, "I'd like to see your manager please," his face stiff with forced politeness. He ran a hand through his hair, dabbed at sweat on his upper lip as he watched the man pick up a phone and make the call. Several minutes later another young man hurried over, an irritated look on his face as he said, "May I help you?"

Reed pulled out his ID. "I'm a detective from Minneapolis, Minnesota!"

The manager eyed him warily. "Yes well, what's this about?"

Reed said, "I need to contact a customer of yours who's been traced to this hotel. Her name is Lorna Lee!"

The young man nervously adjusted his tie, ran a hand over his suit jacket. "Mr. Conners, as you can see we're an upscale hotel. We don't want any trouble here!"

Reed fought to hold his temper. "It's a police matter! Now what room is she in?"

The man cleared his throat. "Well, follow me." Reed was close on his heels as they went into an office and the manager began to punch keys on a computer, clearly agitated at this intrusion into his finely run department. Minutes later, taking an obvious breath of relief he said, "We don't have anyone by that name registered here!"

"Check again, we know she is here!" Reed's voice boomed through the office walls and caused a woman walking up to the desk to stop and look around curiously. The small room was suddenly stuffy and hot as Reed stood braced against a wall. God, he felt like he was going to pass out.

"I repeat, we don't have anyone by that name here! Perhaps you have the wrong hotel!"

Reed swallowed. "Try again buddy, I can get a search warrant and check every room. What would your upscale clientele think of that!" he said with a mean look in his eye.

With reluctance again, the manager paged through another file and finally said, "It looks like Miss Lee was with us, but she left a few days ago!"

"What else?" Reed wiped a hand over his sweating brow.

"Well, she used a fake address," the manager said sarcastically.

Reed stuffed his hands in his pockets; his face, pale and rigid.

"Now if there's nothing else--."

Reed grudgingly thanked the man and turned away to leave, but not before saying, "We'll be in touch!"   Keep the smart asshole on his toes, he thought as he charged out of the hotel.

Goddamn, that meant she must have left right after I went in the hospital, he figured as he got in the Corvette.

"Why the hell didn't I have the police pick her up then?"   He cursed and argued with himself. "For Christ sake, I wasn't even sure if I'd really seen her!"   He groaned as he leaned over and put the key in the ignition. He swore as he shifted gears and headed over to the police station.

"We missed her by a couple of days," Reed said as he walked into Manny's cubicle and sank into a chair.

Manny shoved a pile of papers out of the way after greeting Reed and said, "You think she disappeared again?"

Reed sat up in his chair, an intense look in his eyes as he threw up his hands.

"Homicide has got some news for you on the shooting," Manny said then.

"That was my next question!" Reed got up.

"The chief wants to see you. I hear they got your man." They walked through the faded green hallways and around crowded desks. They dodged people coming and going in the busy place with the foul air of faded humanity ingrained in the space. What now, Reed wondered as they waited for the chief's attention.

"Sit down, glad to see you're up and around, Mr. Conners." He was a man in his fifties, graying and in excellent shape, the police chief's steel blue eyes implied a no-nonsense man. "We picked up the suspect last night. His prints were all over your motel room. Even had your gun in his car!"

Anger burned in Reed's eyes. "Who?" was all he could say.

"A local, a small time drug dealer by the name of Huot. We've been watching him for months!"

Reed looked at the chief curiously as he went on, "Conners, we were aware of you when you were watching his apartment over on Freemont."

"Christ, why didn't you let me know? I was on a case of my own."

"At the time we didn't know who you were. I'm sorry you got caught in the middle of our operation."

"Yeah well, I knew the guy was dealing. Did you run across any information about his girlfriend, Mitzi Grover?"

"She's clean. Took a leave from her job to get away from that sleaze."

There was a trail after all. Reed asked, "Do you know where she is?"

"She went to South Carolina. If I understand correctly, Mr. Conners, you're looking for an acquaintance of hers?"

"Yes, an insurance fraud case."

"Check in with us, we may run across something." The chief stood up. "I'll need you in court this afternoon to identify Huot, right?"

Reed nodded and followed Manny out. They stood together in the hallway as Manny asked, "What'll you do now man?"

Reed exhaled. "Hell, I'm ready to hit the road."

"Let me know if I can do anything from here."

Reed held out his hand to Manny and said, "Remember now, come on up to my place sometime." As he walked back to his car, his shoulder throbbed and his legs were shaking. He fought to keep his fatigued eyes open as he drove back to Betty's apartment. There he collapsed on the couch in her den and was asleep in seconds. Hours later, he awoke as she came in and sat a tray of dinner down on a nearby table.

"Hello handsome, I'm leaving for work at Tony's, so I brought you something to eat." She smiled at her houseguest. Reed sat up, brushed his hair off his face.

"You don't have to wait on me, Betty." He moved his shoulder up and down.

"How does it feel?" Betty sat on an edge of the couch.

"Its better, hell it's been almost two weeks now."

"That's good Reed. Have the Police found out who shot you?"

"Yeah, just some asshole punk. I got in his way." He had never told Betty the complete story about his investigation.

"Thank God, you're okay." Betty got up. "Well, I'm off."

"Betty, I'm going to be taking off tomorrow. I really need to get back to my office up north." Her face fell.

"So soon?"

"I'm through here." Reed reached over for the coffee cup that stood on the tray she'd brought for him.

"Are you well enough to get there on your own?"

"I'll make it." Reed took a sip of the hot coffee and looked around the cozy room he'd spent the last week in. He'd miss Betty and her family.

"I'll be home early tonight and I'll bring a bottle of wine." She left after urging him to eat.

Reed put his feet up on a stool, leaned back on the couch, and picked up the Dallas paper. He wondered how the football game had turned out and turned the pages, pausing now and then to read an article that caught his eye. Suddenly, his feet hit the floor. The paper crackled as he pulled it closer.

A small piece listed under out of state happenings read; "Prisoner on loose!" Reed sat up as he read, "John Thomas, a convicted murderer escapes while serving a life sentence. Spotted, possibly heading south!" Reed sucked in his breath and slumped back against the couch.

How could this happen! He read it again carefully, word for word. His heart pumped furiously as he grabbed the phone and called an acquaintance in law enforcement in the Dallas area. His headache came crashing back as he waited on the phone. It was confirmed; John Thomas, alias J.T. or Jud Thurman had escaped from his prison guards. Reed slammed the receiver down on the phone and the lamp standing on the table tipped precariously towards the edge. He studied the paper again. Thomas was headed south!

Reed sat stone-faced, as the memories of what this man had done came back; cold and cruel facts. It had started when his law school buddy, Tanner Burke had represented Reka Holmes in a divorce suit. Her husband was John Thomas. She'd charged him with physical abuse, adultery, theft, and deception. While the court date was pending, Tanner's secretary Sierra Ames had been killed in a mysterious car accident. That case was never solved. After the divorce was granted, John Thomas served a short term in jail and was released. He had then gained access into an insurance company using false identification. Reed's company. About the same time Reed got orders to re-investigate a claim that had been paid out to a woman named Lindy Lewis, thunder-struck when he realized it was the same Lindy Lewis he had known in college. He'd also gotten orders to investigate the new employee by the name of Jud Thurman. It had all come to a halt when Tanner got shot.

Reed reached for the coffee cup as a stab of loneliness went through his chest and he wondered again, did Tanner figure it out just before John Thomas shot him?

The two buddies, Tanner and Reed had lost touch for a short time during which Reed had sold his ranch and moved to his cabin permanently.

Reed drank the last of the coffee. Now the whole goddamned case was wide open again! John Thomas on the loose and Lindy's whereabouts unknown. He stood up and began to pace. Betty's house was silent, with her at work and the boys at a ball game. Reed left the den and walked around the house. His mind intent and eyes only focused on the moment. He didn't notice the sagging plaid couch, scratched but polished end tables, or the threadbare carpet. In the kitchen he scraped a cracked plastic covered chair out from the chrome table and sat down. He didn't see a gaily-wrapped gift on top of the ancient refrigerator, behind the cereal boxes, that had his name on it. He got up again and paced back and forth.

Goddamn, his head throbbed. He moved his arm and shoulder up and down again, the muscles still aflame. His legs felt like stilts.

Why was John Thomas headed south? Could he have found Lindy's trail too? Had he even traced Reed here on those goddamned computers they had in prisons now for the convicts to play with? Reed cussed. He'd heard John Thomas was a computer genius.

Christ, I've got to get out of here. I can't take the chance of Betty and her family getting hurt!

He went back into the den and gathered his things. Out in the living room, he tore a sheet of paper from a notebook lying on the coffee table. Guiltily, he thought of the night she had planned. Probably a romantic one.

"Betty," he wrote, "I've got to leave tonight to get back in time for an emergency meeting up north. Sincere thanks. I'll be in touch, Reed." He

propped the note up against a napkin holder on the
kitchen table and picked up the phone.

-25-

Lindy drove her black BMW through the southern states, only stopping at out of the way motels to sleep, shower and change clothes. She needed to get as far away from Dallas as fast as possible and she finally relaxed when she crossed into Georgia. This was the last leg of her journey, by afternoon she would arrive at her destination, Hilton Head Island, South Carolina.

The countryside blazed with greenery. Tall stately pines, poplars, ash, and linden trees along with the water oaks, gracefully draped with gray moss lined the highway.

Beautiful, she breathed as she crossed over the long bridges of the International Waterway and approached the island that she'd visited once before with Mitzi. Vibrant flowers and azalea bushes were aflame in the tropical sunshine. Here the trees mingled with palm, palmettos, yucca and the redbud. Bone tired, to keep herself alert until she got to her destination, Lindy talked to herself, remembering Mitzi's history lesson.

"Now Lindy," Mitzi had said in her matter of fact voice years ago, "this place has a lot of history going back to the Civil War. Descendants still reside here holding on to their pieces of land." Lindy smiled as she recalled Mitzi's recital of facts. So like her to have to know everything about a place. They'd been lying on the beach sunning; their skin gleamed with oil.

"This island is eleven miles long and in some places four miles wide," she'd continued, "it's shaped like a high-top shoe. Did you know that? The population is approximately twenty-nine thousand, but over a million people come through every year. This is the summer home for millionaires. Have you seen the mansions that border the island? And you should see the restaurants!" Mitzi had paused to rub more oil on her slim body, rattling on like a travel agent. "This is where I'm going to live when my boy grows up! You know the trade winds keep it blessedly cool here in the summer months, God it gets so damn hot in Dallas."

They had spent a week together, more then ten years ago already. Then things had spun off into years of living their busy lives and not keeping in touch as they had previously. Lindy promised herself to find Mitzi as soon as she was settled and make up for all the time they had missed.

She could smell the salty Atlantic Ocean as she drove down the one main highway that crossed the island. She passed the complex they'd stayed in. This time she was going to be in the plush part of town. She had money. But first, she had to bank that money in a safe deposit box. Inside of thirty minutes she had put it securely away, but left plenty in her purse to play with. If she ran out, she'd just go back and fill her purse again.

Lindy smiled as she remembered Harbor Town and headed to the luxurious gated area bordering the ocean, amidst the world-renowned golf courses and tennis courts. Maybe she'd buy some property and live there, after all, she didn't have a home any more and she had to settle down somewhere, and soon.

Her thoughts were on her past as she drove through the small town, excited to be there again, but also a little lonely to be seeing all this beauty and not having anyone to share it with.

Would Dade Lampart have fit in? J.T. wouldn't have. Reed Conners? He would have. But she'd treated him shabbily. Lindy mused. He was a nice guy, but he wanted to take my money back! I just couldn't hand it over after all the hard work and worry I'd gone through. He had money and the insurance company had loads, Lindy reasoned.

All thoughts of remorse flew out of her head as she arrived at a realty office of a complex of condominiums at Harbor Town. She parked the BMW and left a trail of Christian Dior cologne as she tripped up the Italian marble steps, her high-heeled sandals clicking smartly and her blonde hair windblown and chic.

"I'd like to rent a condo overlooking the ocean," she told the agent.

"Yes, well," he said eyeing her up and down. "I'll be happy to help you, Miss-?"

"Lana, Lana Loylton," Lindy said without batting an eye.

"And how long will you be staying Miss Loylton?"

Hmm--, she hadn't thought about that but answered, "A month, but I might decide to stay longer. I would like an option to stay longer if I decide to?"

"Of course," The man said noting her slim figure encased in an Armani dress. Lindy gave him a flirty smile.

"I'll show you what I have available," he said as Lindy followed him around the tan stucco complex with a red tiled roof. Music flowed from the sidewalk cafés and seagulls squawked as they glided over the water, setting down for a minute or two on the yachts anchored at the pier. The sidewalks were bricked. Expensive boutiques and restaurants lined the water. A huge statue of King Neptune in his loincloth stood holding his spear amongst the trees, pots of flowers and benches. As Lindy looked around the area, she saw people from around the world, engaged in visiting, shopping, drinking and eating. Oh, she was so excited. Now, she would be one of them.

Her condo was on the third floor. When she signed the lease, the realtor had asked, "Will it be a charge?"

"Oh no," Lindy had answered, "I'll pay in cash!" She didn't hesitate when he asked for the money in advance and counted out the bills without a second thought.

A short time later, she stood in her new home decorated in floral peach and pastel green and admired the lovely burnished reed furniture. Glass topped tables graced the white carpeting. Live flowering plants gave off a perfume only found in the tropics. Lindy stepped out on the balcony and found herself in a paradise. Peach striped chaise lounges sat on the marbled floor. She reached over the railing and pressed a magnolia blossom to her nose from the huge tree that leaned in and shaded her patio. She looked at the harbor that was crammed with the expensive crafts and realized she needed more of the right clothes if she wanted to fit in. A shopping trip to those stores that lined the vicinity was in order. She picked up her purse and hurried out in the lovely sunshine.

Maybe she'd give up men for awhile, and just use them to have some fun with, she mused as she shopped. Oh well, she smiled as she fingered the silks and finery in the boutiques, who knew what time would bring. She sighed with resignation. Sometimes they were just too much bother, she murmured under her breath as she slid hangers over the rods.

When she finished shopping late in the afternoon, she had several bathing suits with matching wraps, two dresses, some short sets with the appropriate accessories; shoes, purses and jewelry. The clothes were ridiculously over priced, but what the hell, Lindy smiled, I can afford them!

When she got back to her condo the rooms looked like a cyclone had just gone through, as she paraded around in her new finery. Boxes, bags and tissue paper scattered everywhere. She dressed in a new outfit, fluffed her hair and went downstairs and found a table at an outside cafe that had music. She settled in to enjoy the cocktail hour.

"A margarita please," Lindy told the waiter as she fit a cigarette into a holder she carried for just these times. She tasted the salt on the glass a few minutes later and looked around. Now she was in her element, looking chic in her new clothes, blonde and sexy, and she had money! She lifted her frosted glass and sipped, took a classy drag of her cigarette when suddenly her eyes fell on a familiar face Her glass clinked on the tiled table, her expertly held cigarette fell on the bricks as she gawked in disbelief.

She stood up, waved her arms and yelled over the heads of the other people sitting at tables. Then wound her way through the mass and stood before a woman. "Mitzi!" Lindy exclaimed breathlessly.

The surprised person put her glass down. Then in a second a flash of recognition covered her face as she exclaimed, "Lindy? But where?"

"I just got here!" Lindy said excitedly.

Mitzi jumped up, "I don't believe this. God, it's just too good!" She stepped into Lindy's outstretched arms.

"You haven't changed a bit," Lindy shrieked happily. They stood back and looked at each other and hugged again. The two blondes giggled. "This is such a surprise to see you here Mitzi, I was planning on getting in touch with you to see if you could come." They sat down at the table and leaned in together.

"When did you become a blonde? And brown eyes," Mitzi asked. "It's gorgeous!"

"It's a long story!" Lindy blinked her eyes and fluffed her hair. "I needed a change. What do you think?"

"God, you look good. It's been years."

"Does your Mother still live here?" Lindy asked and leaned back in her chair, and noticed Mitzi's shapely legs encased in the new high-heeled sandals had caught the attention of a nearby table of European men.

"Yes, she does and loves it. I took time off from work. Mark is here too."

"Oh Mitzi, how old is he now?"

"He's sixteen, with raging hormones."

"Oh, I can't believe it. He had just started school the last time we were here."   Lindy flinched at Mitzi's next question.

"Are you still happily married?"

"I was Mitzi, but he died. Almost a year ago now."

Mitzi reached over and clutched her hand. "Oh my God, honey, I'm sorry."

Pain flashed across Lindy's face. She looked out over the ocean for a minute, lost in thought. "We had a good life, but then it ended."   Could she tell Mitzi everything? Maybe later. A waitress brought over Lindy's cigarettes and holder. "Can I bring something from the bar?"

"Yes," Lindy brightened. "A pitcher of margaritas!" The girls pulled their chairs into the table and got ready to do some serious catching up. "Are you still with Rocky Huot?" Lindy asked.

"No!" Mitzi shook her head and raised her eyebrows. "I've left him for good! He slid right back into his old habits. Lost his job and began staying out at night again!"

"Mitzi, here I thought he had straightened out for good."

"Lindy, I found drugs again." Mitzi leaned in closer, "and he was selling the stuff too!"

"No, what did you do?" Lindy asked curiously.

"This time I didn't waste any time. I went to the police, packed up Mark and left!" Mitzi's hand shook as she lifted her glass and drank.

"What an asshole," Lindy said, "after you'd given him another chance too! What are you going to do?"

"I'm not going back until they have him in jail! We're going to stay with my mother."

"You never did marry him, did you?"

"No, I thought about it when he'd straightened out. Now I'm thankful I didn't get that crazy." Mitzi sat up and eyed Lindy, seeing her new look. "Are you rich now?" she asked suddenly

Lindy smiled mysteriously. "I've got some money."

"I'm still poor."

"But you've got Mark."

"Yes, I'm lucky. He's the bright spot in my life. His father still pays support, thanks to Reed Conners, that lawyer friend of yours that scared the shit out of him. What ever happened to him?"

"Oh, he's still in northern Minnesota. I ran into him awhile back."

"Really!" Mitzi's eyes grew large. "After all this time, what did it feel like to see your old college lover again?"

"Hmm-, nice. But, I didn't stay long," Lindy answered evasively.

"Well, have you met anyone?" Mitzi persisted. Lindy picked up a cigarette and inserted it into the holder. She lit it and exhaled a cloud of smoke that hung suspended in the humid air above their heads. Lights blinked on from lamps that lined the harbor as Lindy laughed and said to her friend, "Lord, I've met some dillies! Mitzi, you wouldn't believe it. First, I was going out with a guy that was a murderer and then the next one was gay!"

"What?" Mitzi sat back with a look of horror and then laughter crossed her face.

"Leave it to me. I picked them!" Lindy said and the two girls exploded again in giggles.

"The guy was a murderer Lindy,--What did you do?"

"God, I got far away. And fast!"

"Who did this guy murder?" Mitzi's eyes were huge.

"Well, his wife had hired this lawyer to represent her when she divorced him. He killed both the lawyer, who was Tanner Burke and his secretary. "

"My God! Did he try anything with you?"

"Oh yes! When I realized something was wrong I ran like hell; but he found me just as I was leaving town and chased me on the freeway!" Lindy took a sip of her drink and then a deep drag of her cigarette. "He just about killed me when he tried to run me off the road at ninety miles an hour. Then the weirdest thing happened. I was just about to lose it when a bunch of bikers came along and cut him off. I got away!"

"You mean Harley-Davidson guys?"

"Yes!" Lindy said breathlessly.

Mitzi shook her head. "I always thought they were mean and ruthless."

"I know," Lindy took a deep drag of her cigarette. "In this case, Mitzi they saved my life!" As they talked on twilight descended as the sun disappeared into the water.

"Let me have one of those?" Mitzi said reaching for one of Lindy's cigarettes.

"Hey, you don't smoke. You're a nurse!" Lindy exclaimed, aghast at her friend's action.

Mitzi shrugged and laughed. "Well, sometimes I cheat." She put one in her mouth and coughed when the smoke caught in her throat. "Lindy, how'd you get hooked up with a gay guy?"

Lindy leaned over again, "Listen to this, he needed to get married right away or he would loose the inheritance he'd gotten from his Daddy. We were even engaged!"

"You were!" Mitzi's eyes were large.

"Mitzi," Lindy said, "He gave me this huge diamond ring, and then he went nuts and raped me!"

"My God Lindy, did you go to the police?"

"No, after Betty told me about his scheme and that he was gay, I left!"

"Who's Betty?"

"A woman I'd worked with."

Then what?" Mitzi asked intrigued.

Lindy blew out a breath, "Well, after that, I did what any smart red-blooded American girl would do. I hocked that rock he'd given me and had some fun!" She raised her glass and saluted her friend, "Here's to the men in this world who think the fairer sex is weak!"

"Amen!" Mitzi agreed. The two girls sat and enjoyed the glow of their resumed friendship again, as if a decade of time hadn't gone by. Then Lindy said, "Mitzi get ready. I think we're going to get an invitation to cruise on one of those big boats out there on the water," as two men from a nearby table headed their way.

-26-

"Manny, you got some time to spare?" Reed Conners asked as he paced around Betty's kitchen using her telephone.

"Yeah buddy, what's up?"

"Remember John Thomas? The paper says he got loose while being transferred. He's headed this way."

"No shit! Coming this way?"

"Christ," Reed exhaled, "I thought we had him put away for good. I'm coming down."

Reed hung up the phone and took one last look around Betty's home. This was the second time he had been downtown that day. First to see Manny and the chief, then to attend court in the afternoon to indict the guy who had put a bullet in his shoulder, drug dealer-- Rocky Huot.

He wondered again where Mitzi Grover had disappeared to. She'd been smart to turn that sleaze Huot in and get away.

Reed cussed again at the heavy traffic as the setting sun hit him in the eyes. Don't these fools ever get to where they're going and stay put? He remembered the quiet roads in the north.

Manny was at his desk, dressed in his usual faded jeans and tee shirt. Reed pulled out a chair and turned it backwards, sat and rested his arms over the top.

"Manny, how hard is it to trail someone traveling on a credit card?"

"Not hard at all. Why?"

"Thomas is following me, to get to Lindy!"

"What makes you think that?" Manny asked frowning.

Reed leaned his chin down on his hands and was silent for a minute. "It's a gut feeling! He was obsessed about getting the million dollar insurance money she'd collected. He failed. The asshole doesn't care now, he's broken out of prison and he wants revenge!"

"He got life didn't he?" Manny put his feet up on his desk and leaned back in his chair.

"That's what I mean. He doesn't give a shit!" Reed was silent again. "He's a freak on a computer, no doubt has set up a line of communicators to work with him. Now when he infiltrated the insurance company, Christ, he had a resume that fooled us all.

"That good. A disguise too?"

"Oh yeah, the whole bit. Hair, glasses, clothes."

"How long did he get away with it?"

Reed took a breath and exhaled loudly in the room. "He was with the company a total of five months."

Manny's chair hit the floor with a bang and he asked, "You want me to come in with you on this?"

"I'd appreciate it, man. The feds have this now, but I've got a big stake in it too." Reed got up and began to pace around Manny's cramped office. A deep frown on his face formed as he slapped a fist into his other hand, "Son of a bitch. I'll get that sucker yet!"

Manny shuffled papers on his desk. Reed looked at him.

"Manny, say Thomas has been following me using the trail I've created with my credit cards, he'd know every time I gassed up, where I ate, where I stayed. He'd know where I am."

"Yup," Manny answered. "Exactly!"

"I'm still going on my hunch here, but I'd say he's just about to hit Dallas."

"What about Lindy Lewis?" Manny opened a desk drawer and shoved all the papers in. "I'd bet he knows her whereabouts too."

Reed hesitated, "No--, I don't think so. She's too smart to leave a trail. Remember she's got a lot of cash."

"So what do you want me to do?" Manny looked at Reed questionably.

"Manny, I need a partner. Can you swing it?"

"Hell man, I've got a ton of vacation time and nothing to do. Count me in!"

"I was hoping you would! Okay, here's what we do." Reeds eyes were intent on his thoughts for a minute. "We need a bar. Somewhere off the beaten track. Seedy. Sleazy. No questions asked."

"I've got the perfect spot, Conners. Give me a minute to clear this with the boss." He stood up and went down the hall.

Thirty minutes later as they left the police department in downtown Dallas, Reed said, "Manny I want to start a new trail. Where is this place?"

"It's called the Red Dog. Go down Peachtree to twenty-fourth, turn left and follow that until you get to Mumford. You'll see it on the corner. I've got a stop to make but I'll be there shortly!"

Sweat ran down Reed's back as he walked out into the evening heat. He opened his car door and grimaced in pain as he leaned over and put the key in the ignition. Felt the familiar ache as it flashed through his shoulder and down his arm. He cussed the straight stick clutch every time he had to drive through the heavy traffic.

After twenty minutes he found the bar and parked his car, but not before scanning the neighborhood with dubious concern. He slipped his .38 into his waistband, put a cap over his sandy hair, stuck a toothpick in his mouth and put on his aviator sunglasses. When he checked himself in the rear-view mirror, his five-o'clock shadow had darkened his face. He pulled his shirt out over his jeans to cover the bulge of the gun.

When he opened the door of the Red Dog Bar and walked in, stale smoke, cheap liquor, sweat and fried grease assailed his nostrils. As his eyes became accustomed to the gloom, they were drawn to a huge picture above the bar of a woman's red lips puckered up in a ready kiss. Mexicans, Afro-Americans, and guys just like him wearing western hats, head-bands, jeans and battered boots stood in groups or at the bar. The women clad in halters, tight jeans or shorts. A band tuned up for entertainment on a small stage. The smack of balls from a pool table off to the side split the air. The noise was deafening. He eyed the place through his dark glasses and made his way to the bar.

"What's your poison cowboy?" a low sexy voice asked as he sat.

"Beer." Reed took out a credit card. "Would you start a tab for me? Looks like it's gonna be a long night."

"No problem amigo." When the bartender placed the dark bottle on the bar, Reed raised it hungrily to his lips and downed a big swallow. The cold liquor soothed his burning throat, but a minute later as it hit his stomach; he reeled sideways on his stool. He wiped his mouth with the back of his hand and muttered, "Holy shit, what's in this?" He took another look at the bottle and then the woman bartender. His eyes widened in surprise as she leaned over the bar towards him.

"Too much for you?" She teased him with her dancing eyes. She had short black hair, full breasts and long dangling earrings. She leaned over the bar and put her hand under his chin. Then brought her lips an inch from his. A throbbing began in Reed's lower section. Her cologne was musky and her breath hot.

"Hey Ruby, can't a hard working guy get a drink in this sewer?"

"Hold your horses, peon, can't you see I'm busy!" she yelled good-naturedly. Reed looked with interest as she turned and walked down to the end of the bar amid whistles from the patrons. Her abundant hips and jiggles appreciated. Reed turned as a familiar voice at his side remarked, "That's Ruby, she took over the place when her old man died. She's okay. Puts on quite a show."

Music began and couples took to the dance floor, the air charged with expectations as hungry, hooded eyes from some of the men followed the gyrations of the scantily clothed women.

"What do you think?" Manny asked.

"It'll work. Want a beer?" Reed nodded his head in answer to Manny's question.

"Yeah, perfect."

"You look good," Reed said trying to be heard above the thundering beat of the band. Manny's long hair was loose and hung in strings over his shoulder. His tee shirt and jeans ragged and covered with grease, along with some smeared on his face and hands.

"Yeah, I go with the flow. What's the plan?"

Reed leaned towards Manny. "We're going to do a lot of partying in the next few days. Are you up to it?"

"Hell man, I'm in my element. Hi sugar," he said then to a passing waitress and ran a hand over her hips. She smiled at him. Ruby brought them another beer and gave Reed her inviting look as he took out a cigarette and put it to his lips. Their eyes met as the flame ignited. For a moment, he was taken aback by her brash actions, but also intrigued. He shifted on his stool. The band took a break and his eardrums hummed. After another beer, Reed slid off his stool, "Okay pal, I'm going to split. Meet me here tomorrow, same time."

He signed his check and wound his way through the maze of people and cigarette smoke. Christ, he said in relief as he stepped outside and away from the obnoxious noise, the after taste of the dark beer still heavy in his throat. Relieved seeing his car was still in one piece, Reed got in and slammed the door and felt the quiet. He threw the cap and the dark glasses on the seat and spun out of the parking lot.

Clean Rooms at Budget Prices! Flashed on a sign ahead of him as he drove out of the desolate area. It would do.

"How long will you be staying?" The desk clerk asked.

"A week and I'll pay in cash," Reed said not wanting to give away his address by using a charge card. When he lifted the sheets and laid down with a groan, the last thought that crossed his mind was, okay asshole, come on I'm ready!

***

That same night a lone man clad in faded jeans and jacket, a sweat-encrusted western straw-hat pulled down into a V over his face, had just stolen a black pick-up from an unsuspecting cowhand. A gunrack over the back window held two rifles. He swung the vehicle onto a Dallas highway with a handgun he'd found in the glove compartment next to him on the seat. He was headed straight to a place called Tony's Steakhouse and then Shoney's Coffee Shop.

-27-

L indy and Mitzi lifted their margaritas to their lips and held their cigarettes arched smartly in their hands as they watched the two approaching men. Their eyes met with schoolgirl glee, reminiscent of their years together in college.

"Mi Amore," one said in a heavily accented voice as they hovered at the girl's table. "My brother and I would like to join you." Lindy turned her brown eyes to him and lowered her glass. She looked them over from head to foot.

"Well, I don't know---, what do you think Mitzi?"

Mitzi sucked in her breath and looked doubtful. "We don't have much time."

"Mitzi, you're just not adventuresome! We've got time for one drink," Lindy scolded, taken by their foreign charm.

The two men were handsome, their dark features accentuated by the white linen pants and bright silk shirts they were wearing. Their bare feet encased in Gucci loafers. One of them reached out a hand to Lindy, "My name is Mario and this is my brother, Andre. We've just been enjoying your beauty. Cara Mia, our hearts are beating rapidly."

Oh brother, Lindy thought. Their gold rings, watches and bracelets gleamed in the lamplight.

A waitress stopped by and Mario said, "We'd like a bottle of Dom Perignon."

"Lindy," Mitzi started to protest. Lindy kicked her foot under the table.

"Where are you from?" Lindy smiled demurely and asked, always curious about people. She'd even been accused of being just plain nosey. She swung her sandaled foot out to display her bare leg. Her long skirt was unbuttoned above her knees. Maybe a little too high, she thought now as she glanced down.

She looked up as Mario said, "We're from Florida, but originally from Europe." Mario brought a cigarette to his sensuous lips. His eyes seared hers as he snapped a slim gold lighter. The aromatic smoke hung in the air as he asked, "Have you been here before?"

"Sure, many times," Lindy lied easily and smiled. "So, what brings you two here?"

"We're here to buy and sell." Andre had been sitting quietly and letting his brother do the talking. Now he sat up and uncorked the bottle of champagne the waitress had brought to their table. He filled their glasses and lifted his.

"We need to celebrate. Senoritas!"

"Okay," Lindy said raising hers. "What exactly are we celebrating?"

"Something we've been working on for months!" Everyone clinked their glasses together and began to sip the expensive wine.

"Are you staying here in Harbor Town?" Lindy asked curiously.

"No, we have a place not to far from here. Just a shack really. Whoa--, stop with the questions. Now it's my turn. Where are you from Lindy?" She glanced down at his hand as he put it over hers. His nails were manicured and a diamond sparkled on his right little finger.

"I'm from Chicago," she answered. "But, I've been doing some traveling lately."

"Business or pleasure?"

"You could call it a little bit of each." Lindy lifted the glass of champagne to her lips and took a sip. The sun had set and three blonde sun-tanned men came on stage with guitars and began to play soft Latin music.

”May I have the pleasure of a dance Lindy?" Mario asked as he stood up and reached out his hand. He looked at Andre and nodded his head towards Mitzi.

"Oh, I don't know--," Mitzi said doubtfully looking at Lindy. Andre hadn't been able to take his eyes off her and jumped up hopefully.

"Just one?" he asked taking her hand.

Lindy's heart did a flip-flop when Mario clasped her to him. His spicy cologne enveloped her as he led her smoothly around the moonlit dance floor. Her resolutions to stay away from men lost in the evening breeze. She had to admit to herself, as independent as she liked to be, she really liked a man in her life. She twirled perfectly as Mario swung her in a Tango and her skirt billowed out effectively. She smiled into his eyes as he leaned over her in a dip.

She scanned the floor and checked for Mitzi and Andre. She'd always had to nudge Mitzi to venture out. Lindy was glad she had learned to dance years ago, even though at the time she'd had to drag her husband along. At the sound of the soft guitar Mario pulled her closer and she relaxed into his embrace. The evening ended with promises to meet again the next night.

"Do you think they'll show up Lindy?" Mitzi asked as she smoothed her hair and adjusted her flared skirt. "Andre was so sweet."

"Oh, I think so. Did you notice all the gold? And I know they were wearing Rolex watches!" Lindy and Mitzi hugged and exchanged phone numbers and parted with excitement again at both being in Hilton Head at the same time.

As the next day dawned, Lindy stood on the balcony and watched the sun come up over the ocean. For a few seconds, the world was cast in pink. Tiny clouds formed a network of white lace in front of the glow. A long V-shaped parade of pelicans glided by and gently tipped the white-capped waves.

She dressed in new white shorts and halter, grabbed her sunglasses and hurried out to the beach for a walk. The sun warmed her bare shoulders and soft white sand cushioned her feet. The tide had been in, leaving behind a line of seashells where it had crested, and then receded. She looked awe-struck at the vast expanse of blue water, and wondered what foreign country it reached to. Probably Morocco, she thought. She walked on, the seashells crunching, lost in the beauty of her surroundings and feeling the marvelous freedom.

Caught up in the magnificence, she didn't notice the fog that had begun to roll in. She was several miles out when the sun dimmed and the curtain of gray caught up with her. In a matter of minutes, it enclosed around her. She stopped and watched in horror as it swept past her, spiraling over the beach. She stood still smothered in the close dampness. Everything had disappeared; the sky, the beach and the water, and especially the landmarks. The silence only broken by the crashing waves. Her heart thundered furiously as the Atlantic Ocean seemed to be closing in.

Should she scream? Would anyone hear her? Her clothes hung wet and wrinkled, her hair in wispy strands. As she looked down, she could see her shoes. When she extended her arm out, her fingers disappeared in the heavy mist. She dropped down to her knees in the sand, boxed in on all sides by the heavy gray drape. Her breath caught in her throat as she huddled on the beach, her hands splayed over the seashells. She was lost and alone in a foreign world. It seemed as if hours went by as Lindy sat immobilized in fear, afraid to move, when her mind stumbled back to a childhood memory.

"You always need to have an escape plan in mind to find your way back in case you get lost," she remembered learning from her brothers when they played in the woods as kids. What good was that now? She didn't have one! But, she couldn't sit here and wait, it might take hours, maybe all night for this monstrous curtain of fog to clear!

Gathering her wits about her, she forced herself to think rationally. If she followed the trail of shells along the beach, wouldn't she end up back to where she had started from? She walked forward then panicked, was she headed in the right direction?

"Don't panic, calm down," she whispered to herself. She looked at her watch and saw it had been an hour since she'd left her room.

"Think," she said again, "now if I walk for an hour, I should end up back at the condominium, or if I'm headed in the wrong direction, well, I'll figure out something then." Her heart still thumped. Her breathing in short gasps as she walked along, feeling like any minute she'd break through the wall of white. She checked her watch again and ten minutes had gone by, then thirty, forty and soon, an hour. She stopped and listened. Had she gone too far? Or was she going in the opposite direction after all?

Fearful and exhausted, she sat down on the sand. She'd just stay there and maybe someone would find her. She was just about to give up in desperation when she began to hear faint noises. A car door slammed. A dog barked. Voices echoed through the billowing gray. Then suddenly a wind blew in from across the water and the fog cleared. Then the boardwalk came into view. She ran the last few steps and collapsed safely in her room, put on a robe and went out on her balcony to sit in the sun. Warmed, she began to relax. But, suddenly her life seemed alien to her.

What was she doing here anyway? She was so alone. Mitzi and Mario were forgotten, as she started to miss her home. The way it used to be when her husband had been alive and the two of them happily renovated the house. She lay in a chaise lounge, her thoughts far away. The air mixed with salt from the ocean and the perfume of magnolia blossoms.

Lindy had been raised in a large family. There had never been a shortage of food, but, a shortage of love and affection. Lindy's recollection of growing up was painful and lonely until she'd gotten older. A frown crossed her face as she came back to the present and began to worry.

What about her money! She knew she tended to be extravagant and what would she do when it ran out? She daydreamed back in time.

If things had turned out that time she had gone to Hollywood, she probably would be famous by now! She'd never gotten over that. After saving money and taking time off from college, she had ridden a bus into the town of her dreams where she was going to be another Loretta Lynn. But, not knowing the right people to see and the right places to go, she'd had to give up and come home. Sadly, she put her guitar and songbooks away in a back closet.

Lindy pulled the robe closer as she sat out in the sun on her patio in Hilton Head. Then remembered the time when a seemingly respectable looking couple had promised her she could earn big money being a model. Again, she'd saved her money and paid to have a book of photos of herself ready to start an exciting new career. That had fizzled too when Lindy found out they were a front for a prostitution ring. She'd finally given up all thoughts of glamour and went to work as a waitress in a hamburger joint intent on finishing college. There she'd met Reed Conners.

She sat up with a new thought. Maybe she'd give the money back to his insurance company after all, go back home and learn to live in the small safe community.

Lindy looked up at the southern sky then just as a star flashed across the horizon. She leaned back and gazed in awe. Well--, maybe she wouldn't go home yet. Mario seemed promising. And then she had all those new clothes to wear, but she'd give it some thought tomorrow.

-28-

Reed awoke early the next morning in his room at the budget motel. He threw the covers off, stood up and stretched. In the shower, hot water and soap suds splashed on the worn linoleum floor in the bathroom as life cursed back into his veins. That, and the fact that John Thomas was on the loose.

Son of a bitch, reverberated against the walls as Reed muttered. When I get my hands on you again sucker, there won't be enough left of you to put back in prison!

It was a waiting game! He stepped out of the enclosure with a skimpy towel barely covering his big frame and stalked around the room looking for his pack of cigarettes; leaving puddles of water on the floor. Back in the bathroom, taking his first drag of the smoke, he stood in front of the mirror and surveyed himself. The lines and crevices on his face highlighted by the harsh overhead bulb. He leaned in closer, and then stepped back. He didn't look any better from a distance. Realizing he was looking at his fiftieth birthday soon, he suddenly felt old. Alone and old. He shaved, brushed his teeth and combed his hair, not before grimacing at the gray that had somehow managed to spring out, unbeknownst around his temples and sideburns. As he dressed he surveyed the room. It was grim.

Christ, he thought, except for my house up north, I don't have anything in my life that's real. No woman, not even a dog or cat that gives a shit if I come home or not. His blue eyes held a sadness that no amount of laughter had ever been able to erase. He sat down in the shabby arm chair and reached for another cigarette. Hunger burned a hole in his stomach, but he was in no hurry to find a place for breakfast. He sighed. Maybe, he should have married Joanne years ago. She was a daughter on a neighboring ranch that was in love with him, but he didn't feel the necessary sparks. Well, maybe things would have changed. At times, he wished he had a faithful warm body to sleep next to. But, would she have understood his independence? His absent mindedness? Maybe, maybe not. He knew he could be an ornery cuss.

But what the hell. He'd been a loner since he was sixteen years old, when his parents had been killed in a plane accident. He was the only child of successful ranchers. Their Mexican foreman and his wife had stayed on in the house and taken care of him until he'd finished high school and college, and was old enough to take over. He sat back in the chair; put his head back on the top and sighed with resignation. The loneliness had started then and had shadowed his life. In college, he'd met Tanner Burke, and then Lindy Lewis. They'd become his family until time and distance had separated them, each going their own way to pursue their careers. Tanner was dead now. When Lindy had come back in his life, he'd had a faint glimmer of small hope, but that had gone sour too.   God,   he   was lonely.

He forced himself out of the chair, went out and found a restaurant. Each day dragged, but with a mounting tension. Reed sensed John Thomas was getting nearer. Every evening he met Manny at the Red Dog and slugged down beer and waited, always using his charge card to pay. Eventually Thomas would pick up his trail. They'd become familiar faces around the bar, and Ruby's apparent offers became more enticing. Back at the motel he picked up the phone. When Betty answered, he was taken back at her quick intake of breath when he greeted her.

"Reed Conners, I'd given up on you," then with a catch in her throat she asked, "How are you handsome?" He had to admit, it felt good to hear her voice.

"I'm fine, Betty. How are you and the boys?"

"We're okay. We miss you though." Reed lay back on his bed and pulled a pillow under his head.

"I'm surprised I found you at home. Aren't you working at the coffee shop today?"

Betty laughed. "I took the day off. The boys are in school so it's heavenly around here."

Reed stretched his legs. "How are things at Tony's?"

Betty blew out a breath. "That's why I took the day off. It's busy and crazy as usual. Did you get home all right?"

Reed hesitated. Now he had to tell her he'd been in town all along. "I didn't leave Betty. I'm still here."

"What?" Betty questioned. "Why? Why didn't you stay here then?"

Oh shit, he didn't want to hurt her. "Well, things got canceled up north, and the company wanted me to check something else while I was here. I just got a cheap room."

"You could have come back here Reed."

"I know Betty, but I just thought I better not clutter up your life any longer."

"Reed, how can you say that?"

"I know. I'm sorry." Now he felt like hell.

"Okay handsome. You can make it up to me. Come on over and have a cup of coffee."

"Now?" Reed sat up on the bed.

"I can't think of a better time, can you?"

"Well, if you're sure. I can be there in thirty minutes."

"Okay handsome," Betty repeated.

He heard her clunk down the receiver. As he walked out of the dismal motel room, he had to admit again, it felt good to have a woman really wanting to see him.

A whiff of a delicate perfume hit his nostrils as Betty opened the door for him. She pulled him in the room and clasped him in a hug. She'd dressed in cut-off jeans, a bright red tee-shirt and tennis shoes. Her blonde hair was bunched on top her head. They stood together with their bodies yielding to each other's touch and then just as quickly parted. Neither of them knowing where to put their feelings.

"I've got the coffee ready," Betty said as they walked into the kitchen. She opened the oven door and peeked in. The most wonderful smell of cinnamon escaped into the room and mixed with the aroma of coffee. "The rolls will be ready in a minute."

Reed's stomach growled as he sat down at her table and reached for the mug she handed him. He took a swallow and looked around. The house smelled of Pine-Sol cleaner. The appliances and windows sparkled, although they were old and outdated. The curtains were white with gold fuzzy dots with perky tie-backs. The cupboards had been freshened lately with white paint. Today the gray and chrome kitchen set looked brighter with a pot of sunflowers sitting over a lace scarf. Betty turned down the radio that sat on the counter and Garth Brooks' voice faded into the background.

"It's good to see you Reed. How is your shoulder?" Betty gathered plates and knives from the cupboard.

"Not too bad now. Just a little stiff." He leaned back in his chair and crossed a booted foot over his knee.

"Have you gone back to the doctor?"

"Nah, I'm fine. How are the boys doing in school?" Betty put the fresh rolls on the table and sat down.

"Fortunately, their grades are good and they don't seem to be in any trouble. You never know now days. Taste these."

"Hmm-- delicious," Reed murmured as the warm morsel teased his taste buds. A comfortable minute went by as they sat silently. He looked at her with interest. Her heart-shaped face was accentuated with dimples and thick lashes framed her blue eyes.

"I've missed you Reed. I'm sorry, but I have to be honest," she said smiling.

Oh Christ. Reed's hand shook as he lifted the mug of coffee to his lips and a familiar tightness fanned out in his groin. He stood up and moved to Betty's chair.

"Come here," he murmured and reached for her hand. For a minute Betty looked surprised, then smiled and stepped into his arms and their lips met. Their tongues searched, and then finally found the need in each other. He scooped her up in his arms and headed for her bedroom. The soft strains from Elvis singing Blue Moon, echoed softly from the white plastic radio on the kitchen counter as Reed kicked the bedroom door shut.

-29-

Lindy snuggled between the silk sheets on her bed in her new condo in Harbor Town. She'd left the French doors to the balcony open overnight and the cool ocean breezes swept through the rooms. Morning doves chanted just outside, joined with the copycat answer of the mockingbird. The telephone awakened her and she sat up and looked around. For a moment she was lost in her surroundings until she threw the covers off and picked up the receiver—recognizing her friend's voice.

"Mitzi, it's good you called," she ran a hand through her hair and went on, "I missed you yesterday."

"I had a job interview! When I finally got home, I was too stressed and worn out to do anything but go to bed."

"Are you seriously thinking about staying here in Hilton Head?" Lindy blew out a breath.

"Well you know, if I can find something that pays enough to live on, I might. Mom wants us to!"

"Wouldn't it be great if we both stayed? All this beauty and warm weather!"

"Wow, it really would! Mom took Mark to the beach and then later, they're going out to eat. Do you want to get together today?"

"Let's meet for lunch." Lindy stood up and stretched.

"Okay," Mitzi said with laughter, "I need to unwind. In a couple of hours then?"

Lindy lay back in her bed, and again the horror of being lost in the fog the day before came back to haunt her. She shivered and pulled the covers up to her chin. Something about it had left her with an uneasy feeling.

Was it some new impending danger? "Well Lindy Lewis, get up and do something!" she scolded herself. She stepped into the shower, shampooed her hair and shaved her legs. She pulled another new outfit off a hanger and slipped into a coral and peach long skirt and skimpy top. She put in her contacts, applied her make-up and styled her hair. A short time later, pleased with her appearance, she felt better. Sure of herself. She walked downstairs and through the lobby of the condo's office and smiled at the same man she'd rented her rooms from.

"Good morning, Miss Loyalton," the trim well dressed salesman said, "Everything okay for you?"

"Wonderful," Lindy smiled. "You can call me Lana."

He gave her an admiring look. "Lana, did I tell you we have limousine service available for our guests? Free of course."

"Really, well I'll certainly remember that!" Lindy smiled at him and walked out into the blazing morning sun. Just my style, she thought.

The day was glorious, as the air fresh with the ocean scent fanned over the shore. Cobblestone sidewalks glistened with dampness. Tubs of flowers bloomed everywhere cascading down the sides of containers; the reds, pinks, and oranges, brilliant to the eye. Lindy inhaled the heady fragrances as she walked along gazing into the shop windows, sidestepping other morning strollers. Maybe she would stay here too. Become one of the natives.

"Mitzi," she called out then as she came to the outdoor café where they'd arranged to meet. Her friend was sitting at a table and waved. They hugged and sat down. Mitzi was tall and slim, naturally blond, with a Scandinavian accent. She'd been raised in the southern states, as her father had been in military service. The sun shimmered on the two blondes as they sat at the table in their gaily colored dresses.

"So what have you been doing?" Mitzi asked Lindy as they adjusted their chairs and ordered from the waitress.

Lindy reached in her purse and took out a pack of cigarettes. "God Mitzi," she said as she laughed nervously, "I went for a walk on the beach yesterday and as I was walking along enjoying the scenery, suddenly everything was covered with this fog! I couldn't see a thing. I was lost and I didn't know where the hell I was!"

Mitzi sat up in her chair as Lindy sucked in her breath. "Mitzi, I panicked," she whispered as she lit a cigarette and put it in the holder. She inhaled and blew out a trail of smoke.

"What did you do?" Mitzi's eyes grew larger.

"Mitzi, I was really scared, but I remembered what my brothers had told me when we were kids about what to do if you got lost, and I had enough sense to turn around and follow the trail of seashells along the waters edge.

"Lindy," Mitzi wailed, "I forgot to tell you the fog and these coastal storms come in fast. They can be dangerous!"

"I found out!" Lindy grinned then and changed the subject. "Let's order a margarita, okay?" Mitzi smiled and said, "That sounds heavenly to me."

After several hours of catching up amid giggles, a pitcher of margaritas and a seafood lunch, Mitzi asked, "What are you going to do when the money runs out from that engagement ring you hocked? The one you got from that gay guy!"

Lindy's face sobered as Mitzi went on, "Why don't you look for a job here Lindy, the town is full of ritzy hotels and restaurants. With all your experience you wouldn't have any trouble."

Lindy shuttered. What a sobering thought! But, she had over a million dollars!

Should she tell Mitzi?   She was her close friend. Lindy hesitated for a minute, and then made up her mind.

"Mitzi," she said innocently, "you remember my house don't you?"

"Of course. That mansion you guys slaved over for years to fix up."

Lindy took another drag of the cigarette. "Well, after Robert died everything went wrong with it!"

"Like what?" Mitzi asked curiously.

"It would have crumbled and fallen down eventually."

"What do you mean, fallen down?"

Lindy shuddered, "It was full of carpenter ants!"

"Ants!" Mitzi's face was incredulous.

"Yes ants… in the roof, walls; the whole house!"

It was Mitzi's turn to shudder. She gulped, "Well, Lindy what did you do?"

Lindy straightened up and said soberly, "I burned it down!"

"What?" Mitzi gaped at her friend.

"Well Mitzi, what else could I do?" Lindy had an indignant look on her face and went on, "I had good insurance on it!"

"But you can't do that!"

Lindy looked at her friend's face and started to giggle. Suddenly peals of laughter rang out, startling the other customers.

Lindy adjusted her skirt and wiggled her toes in her sandals. "I know it's dishonest, but I had no other choice!"

"You didn't get caught?"

"Well kind of," Lindy answered as a frown crossed her face. Maybe she'd made a mistake in confiding in Mitzi. Her and her questions.

"How did you do it," Mitzi whispered?

What the heck Lindy thought to herself, she's my best friend. "When I was redecorating that last room; the paint thinners ignited the cleaning rags and immediately spread. Within minutes it was totally engulfed in flames!"

For a second Mitzi looked at Lindy in horror. Then they giggled again.

"Oh my God, you pulled it off," Mitzi said wiping her eyes. "Weren't you scared?"

"Damn scared!   And then the wait for my insurance check was horrible!"

"Give me a cigarette, Lindy, this is making me nervous."   Lindy looked at her friend. The momentary doubt she'd had disappeared. She might as well tell Mitzi everything. She pulled her chair closer.

"Reed knows!"

"He found out?" Mitzi whispered.

"It turned out; he had closed his law practice and worked as an investigator for an insurance company."

"Oh God Lindy!"

"Listen to this, he investigates possible fraudulent claims," Lindy went on, "and, checks out new employees for the company."

"Well, what happened?   Did he arrest you?" Mitzi asked.

"It was an odd set of circumstances." The afternoon sun was high in the sky casting a brilliant glow over the ocean. Waves beat lazily against the beach as tourists lay on their gaily colored towels or sat around in groups sunning themselves. Mouth-watering aromas from the restaurant's kitchen hung in the moist air. Lindy's eyes swept over the area and came back to Mitzi's face. She leaned in closer and spoke in a low voice.

"I didn't know the extent of it until much later. Reed was following a man, a con named John Thomas. I met him when he posed as the insurance adjuster who delivered my check. He was going by the name Jud Thurman or J.T. Later, I started dating him. Not realizing his plan was to wine and dine me and steal the money. It was a set up!"

Mitzi's face was rosy from the excitement, but managed to ask, "How much was that check?"

"One million dollars!" Lindy whispered.

"A million dollars!" Mitzi shrieked.

"Shh-," Lindy said, putting a finger over her lips. The girls looked around then, sobering.

Mitzi's eyes were still large. "Lindy, this is incredible!"

"I know." Lindy said and went on, "I kind of fell for J.T., but when I discovered who he really was I got scared. He damn near killed me on the freeway when I was trying to get away from them. With the help of some bikers I got away!"

"There was someone with J.T.?"

"A black man was driving the big red car!" Lindy picked up another cigarette and stopped to take a sip of her drink.

"When did you see Reed?"

"I got off the freeway and went into a casino. I thought I could hide in the crowds and that's when

I ran into Reed." Lindy's breath caught as she lit the cigarette and placed it in her holder.

"Oh God," Mitzi murmured.

"There he sat at a black-jack table. And by then I was so glad to see a friendly face," Lindy said, then continued. "We had a drink and I told him I had to stop because I had a migraine." Lindy smoked in silence for a few seconds.

"Reed said he was working on something, and that his best friend Tanner Burke had just been killed. He said I could stay at his cabin. Remember the one you visited?"

"Yes, the one with the cozy little lake." Mitzi took another cigarette and inhaled like an old pro. "He still has that?"

Suddenly feeling chilled, Lindy pulled her long skirt around her bare legs. "He sold his ranch and fixed up his cabin and lives there all year long. You should see it now Mitzi, it's beautiful! He had said he'd be back in a few days and I should wait for him. I was there almost a week and I hadn't heard from him. Then one day as I was sitting out on the dock I looked up as I heard footsteps and saw J.T. and this black man coming towards me. They'd found me!" Lindy shivered, remembering the horror.

"My God!" Mitzi's hand flew to her mouth. "What happened?"

"All this time Reed had been just behind J.T., and finally followed him to the cabin. Apparently, J.T. had found out where I was. There I sat like a pigeon! But before I knew what happened, Reed and the cops showed up and captured J.T. and his buddy."

"This is unbelievable Lindy!"

"I know it sounds like a B movie, doesn't it?"

The waiter came by their table then and asked, "Ladies, can I refresh your drinks?"

"Yes!" The girls said in unison.

"Then Reed let you go?" Mitzi questioned after he left the table.

"Well, we spent a few days together. It was so nice, we made love!"

"Wasn't it kind of strange, you know after so long?" Mitzi asked after seeing the far away look in Lindy's eyes.

"Yes--no, it was just like old times. Better even."

"Then what!"

"He told me he was shocked when he found out I was involved in the insurance investigation he'd been working on."

"I bet he was." Mitzi leaned in closer to Lindy. "Was he mad?"

Lindy looked out at the ocean again. Hesitated for a minute. "No--, funny thing," he said,

"Give the money back and I'll help you with the charges. He is a lawyer you remember."

"Lindy, I don't think he ever got over you, you know."

Lindy took a drink of the fresh margarita. Felt the cold spun ice and tequila slide down her throat. She swung her foot out from under the table, admired her high-heeled sandals.

"Hmm- maybe. Well, his plan sounded like a good idea at the time. I even promised, but, when I got in my car the next morning, the money safely in my underwear bag, I just had to get away from there."

"I'm surprised he didn't put you in handcuffs or something? He let you go by yourself and he didn't follow you?"

"Well no, he had to go to the funeral for his friend Tanner early that morning and he trusted me to wait for him at his house. We'd agreed, he'd drive to Minneapolis and we'd go to the insurance company and I'd return the money."

"Lindy, why didn't you?"

"Well, after he left I just couldn't do it! All that lovely money. So I just got in my car and drove off!" Lindy smiled. "That bad witch made me do it!"

"You've still got it?" Mitzi whispered with astonishment on her face. They both jumped then as a man's voice said, "Hello, Miss Loyalton." Lindy looked up and smiled at the man from the realty company. "Beautiful day, isn't it Lana!"

"Just gorgeous." she answered sweetly.

Mitzi sat speechless as they watched him walk away. "Lana Loyalton," she gasped?

Lindy chuckled. "I changed my name, just in case."

"God Lindy," was all Mitzi could say. She gulped her drink.

"Let me tell you the rest, it gets really bizarre. I drove and finally ended up in Dallas. I had just gotten out of my car to go into a restaurant and I was mugged. My car, the money, everything was gone. I had to go to work! Then on a hunch, I placed an ad in the newspaper, offered a reward."

Mitzi had begun to chew on a thumbnail as Lindy continued, the words coming out easier now after the drinks. "Can you believe this Mitzi, a guy turned up with the car! Of course, he didn't know he'd been driving around with a million dollars hidden in the seat!"

"It was still there?"

"Yes!" Lindy smiled again.

"What did you do?" Mitzi's voice squeaked as she stared at her friend.

"Well, I left town and here I am!"

"I just can't believe this Lindy. You were always so quiet, so reserved."

"Well, it was that damn house that started this." Her eyes clouded.

"Aren't you afraid?"   Mitzi asked with a worried frown on her face.

"Well--, in a way. I saw Reed in Dallas. He was hurt."

"What do you mean? Where?"

"Mitzi, I had to go to a hospital, I wasn't feeling good. And when I left there, he was being wheeled in on a stretcher. He didn't see me though."

"Really, what was wrong?"

Lindy said, "He'd been shot, but I called a little later and they said he was going to be okay. God, I was so relieved to hear that."

"Do you think he knew you were in Dallas?"

Lindy shook her head, "Maybe--I don't know what else he'd be doing there!"

"So, what are you going to do?"

Lindy smiled and fluffed her hair, just as a sleek yacht slid into the marina. Two men got off and started towards their table waving, "Lindy, Mitzi, join us!"

-30-

Reed and Betty lay tangled in the covers of the bed, her head rested on his shoulder as their breathing calmed. A sliver of late afternoon sun peeked through the partially closed window shade.

"Am I hurting you Reed?" Betty asked sitting up suddenly remembering his gunshot wound, then covered her chest with the sheet.

"No--" Reed said lowering it and running a fingertip over a nipple. Her breath caught as his hand explored the newly discovered planes of her body, his lips exciting her secret erotic senses.

They made love again and this time as they lay spent, dampness drying on their bodies, Reed fell asleep. Betty guiltily checked the time and saw she still had several hours before the boys returned from school. She laid back and quietly moved into Reed's embrace.

In his slumber, Reed tightened his hold; put his face in her hair. His body relaxed finally and she smiled as a loud snore rattled the room. Just as suddenly as Reed fell asleep, he awoke and sat up. His hair tousled, and his two hundred pound frame sagging the mattress as he thought with alarm, what the hell had he done!

He searched Betty's face for a sign of remorse? But she smiled. He stood up, searching through the clothes they'd hurriedly shed. He found his shirt and cigarettes. Leaning back against the headboard, he lit one and inhaled deeply. Handing it to her, they smoked in silence, each lost in their own thoughts.

"Will I see you again Reed?" Betty asked hesitating, as she stood up and reached for a robe on a nearby chair.

"Do you want to?"

"Silly, do you have to ask?" She turned and began walking out of the bedroom then asked, "Would you like some iced tea?" Reed went into the bathroom, ran water over his face and got dressed. When Betty returned, ice cubes clinked against the sides of the glasses as they sat side by side on her bed.

"You know, I didn't get a chance to tell you Reed, a stranger has been around asking about you." Reed's body stiffened, blood surged to his head.

"When?" he barked.

Betty jumped at the sharpness in his voice. She looked at him strangely. "He's been around a couple of times. He asked the bartender if he'd seen you. Described you too."

"What did the bartender say?" Reed's senses flared.

"Tommy has a closed mouth. He just said he couldn't be sure. I saw this man in the coffee shop too."

"Describe him Betty." She looked at Reed's intense face and went on, "Well let's see. Medium height. Wiry. Brown hair and a mean look in his brown eyes. Who is this guy?"

Reed sat stone-faced. His mind racing. So he was here! Thomas was in Dallas and close! Reed stood and walked the length of the small bedroom with a glass of iced tea in his hand.

"When was the last time you saw this guy Betty?" She straightened the covers on the bed as Reed leaned against the doorframe.

"The day before yesterday at Tony's," Betty answered.

A streak of adrenalin shot through Reed's body. How soon until Thomas showed up at the Red Dog! Abruptly Reed turned to go, "I've got to check on something Betty, but I'll call you." She walked with him to the door, he gave her a quick kiss on the lips and left.

The slime is here, echoed through Reed's head as he raced out of Betty's parking lot, and punched in Manny's number on his newly acquired cell-phone.

"Talk," was Manny's greeting which matched his terse personality.

"Manny, we've hit pay dirt! Thomas is here!"

"Where?"

Reed shifted the Corvette into fourth gear. "My old stamping grounds, Tony's Steakhouse and Shoney's Coffee House. Asked about me!"

"What's the plan Reed?"

"He's just behind us. We'll see him soon!"

"Okay buddy. Usual time tonight?"

Reed clicked off the phone and sub-consciously ran a hand over his shoulder as he sped through the streets of Flower Mound, Texas. He returned to his motel room, showered, turned on the television and tried to concentrate on the news. He had to be calm and alert. His fingers tightened on his shoulder holster. He took the .38 automatic out, checked the clip and snapped it back in place.

Finally, it was time to meet Manny for their stakeout at the Red Dog where Reed had created a facade of a stranger of questionable means, friendly, but, dangerous to mix with the crowd. He dressed in faded jeans, adjusted his shoulder holster, and slipped a knife in his pocket. In the car, he jammed the cap on his head, and aviator sunglasses on his face.

The Red Dog was crowded and cloudy with smoke as he pushed the door open. Jerry Lee Lewis' gravelly voice and abrasive piano wailed on the juke box. The air-conditioner had apparently blown again, but it didn't seem to bother anyone. Scantily clad cocktail waitresses pushed their way through the people, precariously balancing their ice-laden glasses on trays. Reed eyed the crowd as he made his way to the bar and by now, the strong beer had become a welcome treat to his taste buds. He turned now and then to greet an acquaintance, return a slap on the back. Ruby smiled her suggestive greeting and asked, "Your usual?"

"Yep, run a tab," he said and slid his credit card on the bar towards her. He leaned in and leered at her as she bent to the low refrigerator. They'd become friends and talk came easily as they harmlessly flirted with each other. Reed drank thirstily out of the bottle and turned to look over the crowd.

Manny inched his way over to him and picked up the bottle that was already waiting. His usual grease stained jeans and cut-off shirtsleeves attire, a familiar look now. Both men moved down to the end of the bar, to a better vantage point.

Outwardly, they looked like the rest of the hot, tired blue-collared crowd. Most of them of questionable origins, Reed guessed. Tension filled the air tonight as the heat accelerated with the deep throbbing music.

"What do you think?" Manny asked as he wiped his drooping mustache with the back of his hand.

"Too soon," Reed answered as his eyes swept the place behind his dark glasses. He kept a hand on the sweating beer bottle and began stroking it up and down.

"Will you recognize him?" Manny raised his beer, eyes intent on Reed's face.

"Oh yeah," Reed answered, "Unless he comes in dressed as a hooker or something." He raised his beer.

"You know what to do then don't you?" Manny laughed.

"Tell me. I've got my own ideas though."

"Hell man, a quick feel and if he's got a crank taped up in his panties, you'll know right off." Manny slapped the bar. They took their time and drank beer, watching the door. But outside of the usual regulars, no one new showed up.

"Ruby, get that air fixed," Reed said as he left.

"Sure, if you can find me someone to do it. They're weeks behind and charge two hundred bucks an hour!"

"Must be the business to be in." Reed flashed her a smile and gratefully stepped outside, the air a welcome relief, but only a few degrees cooler. The next morning, he called the police department in northern Minnesota to bring them up to date on the case.

"Conners," the chief said, "where the hell have you been? For Christ's sake, we lost track after you left the hospital. I've got some bad news for you!"

"What?" Reed exhaled nervously.

"We've had a hell of an ice storm and your neighbors called here trying to find you. The roof on your house caved in from the weight of the build-up."

"How bad?" Reed managed to ask.

"Well, I think you better get back now!"

-31-

Lindy and Mitzi watched as Mario and Andre strolled over to their table in the outdoor café, their tanned bodies clad in brief swimming trunks and shirts slung casually over their shoulders.

"Ciao," Mario said dripping with Italian charm and reached for Lindy's hand, then kissed it. Taking off his dark glasses he asked, "`Senorita's, would you join us on our yacht today?"

Lindy smiled into his eyes and motioned to Mitzi as she said, "We'd love to."

"Well, I don't know," Mitzi said anxiously and checked her watch.

"We'll have you back early," Mario said. Andre looked at Mitzi longingly.

"Are you sure?" she said, "I told Mark I would be back before evening." Looking at Andre, she added, "He's my son."

"Don't worry, Mitzi," Mario said as he put his arm around Lindy's waist as she stood and gathered her things.

"Come on Mitzi, we'll watch the time," Lindy added and was pleased her new outfit had matching shorts underneath the long skirt when they walked out to the pier.

The yacht was huge and gleaming white and was named Amour. Mitzi sucked in her breath at the lavishness, but followed Lindy's casual actions and hid her eyes behind dark glasses as the men showed them around the house on water.

Lovely carpets graced the floors. Mahogany furniture and accessories complimented the silk covered walls. Beige and white, the color theme. The bedroom suites were a dream. The back of the yacht held an open deck with green and white striped furniture. A white linen cloth covered a dining table set.

No paper plates and coolers here, Lindy chuckled to herself. They spent the afternoon cruising on the ocean, sipping wine and then at sundown, Mario set out a seafood dinner. No one spoke of leaving, not even Mitzi, who had grown quite relaxed to Lindy's surprise as they danced under a blanket of stars. Finally, being just a little bit tipsy and knowing her weakness for situations just like this, Lindy untangled herself from Mario's arms and asked him to take them back to shore.

They ended the evening with kisses and promises.

Lindy's next few days were filled with excitement and fun. She'd kept her BMW safely in the garage at the condominium and now availed herself to the luxury of using the limousine service supplied by the Harbor Town complex. She was sure, she was known as a girl about town, traveling in style, dressed in her fine clothes. Her daily routine started with a walk on the beach, and today, grabbing her plaid baseball cap and dark glasses she started off, but mindful of the sky after that one episode she'd had earlier in the week.

The sun broke over the horizon and gentle breezes chased the morning dew off the palm trees that lined the dunes. Seashells crackled under Lindy's feet as she walked. Her fair skin had taken on a golden hue, and her blonde hair had gotten lighter.

After completing her two-mile trek, she showered and dressed, called Reno, the limo driver and asked him to pick her up. She had a stop to take care of first and then she planned to seek out a restaurant where she had heard hordes of people gathered each day. To see and be seen. "Good morning Miss Loyalton," Reno said as he opened the car door for her. He was of Spanish decent and in his late thirties.

"Good morning Reno," Lindy replied as she settled in the seat and arranged her skirt. Reno gave her a wide smile, showing perfect teeth. He touched his chauffeur's cap and pulled it lower over his face as he closed the door. His white shirt and tight trousers accentuated his slim hips and broad chest. The breeze swirled his spicy cologne in the air. The long white car purred smoothly as they left the parking zone that led onto Main Street. Huge magnolia trees, water oaks laden with moss, and stately pines bordered the cobblestone drive.

"Reno, I have to make a stop at the Plaza Bank," Lindy said as she searched in her purse for her safe deposit key.

"Then would you take me to the Hilton Head Diner?" Soft music purred from the speakers as the air-conditioner hummed. Lindy sat back in the seat and put on her dark glasses.

"I'll just be a few minutes," Lindy said then as he brought her to the bank. In the vault, she counted out a stack of one hundred dollar bills and tucked them in her billfold. Then lovingly fingered the rest of the bundles. She would have to take time to count her money soon. See how much she had left.

When she came out of the vault a man stood near the counter, the same one she remembered who had been there when she went in. He ducked his head down quickly to something he was writing.

As Lindy walked out of the bank, she glanced back just before the door closed and saw him walking towards her. Fast! She hurried into the limousine and snapped at the driver to get going. As they pulled away from the curb, she looked back through the darkened window. The man was getting into a shiny black sedan.

Was it just her imagination or had she seen him before?

The Diner restaurant was in an up-scale hotel. The host sat Lindy at a table by a window and placed a menu in front of her. The people around her were elegantly dressed in designer cruise wardrobes. Gold gleamed on their wrists and fingers and the air was delicately laced with expensive colognes. Taking her cigarettes out of her purse and instead of using her Cricket lighter, Lindy reached for the book of matches on the table. She ordered an omelet and dawdled over her meal, then a man's voice said, "Pardon me lady, may I join you for coffee?"

A tall man, dressed in tan shorts and a white Tommy Hilfiger tee shirt stood next to her table. Not waiting for an answer, he pulled out a chair and sat down. He caught the eye of a waiter and within seconds a cup and saucer was set down and filled.

Lindy sucked in a breath. It was the same man she'd seen at the bank!

"Are you enjoying the island?" he asked casually.

"Excuse me?" she replied warily.

He lifted his cup of coffee and tasted it after stirring in cream and sugar. "Are you here for long?"

He looked to be in his sixties. A good-looking man, with deep-set blue eyes. Laugh lines crinkled around them as he gazed at her. His face was tanned and his features chiseled. A birthmark peeked out from under his hair that fell over his forehead.

Lindy sat back in her seat, and even though her nerves were quaking, she managed to ask, "Why are you following me?"

"Ahh--a fine looking woman like you, you shouldn't be traveling by yourself. You need someone to show you around town," he said avoiding her question.

"I get around just fine, thank you!" Lindy answered in a huff.

"I bet I could show you places you don't know about." He reached for her hand.

She stood up and jerked her hand back and said, "You've got a lot of nerve. I prefer to pick my own company!"   She left some bills on the table, but felt his eyes burn into her back as she walked away. She went to the ladies room and called Reno. Then dropped into an easy chair and clasped her purse to her chest as an uneasy feeling edged through her chest. She remembered that covert look on his face as he had watched her earlier.

Who was this man? Did he suspect who she was? She stared in the mirror. She didn't look anything like Lindy Lewis anymore. Lindy had been a brunette with short hair. Now she was blonde with a classy hair-do. Brown eyes instead of blue. Wearing make-up and expensive clothes instead of the denims she'd lived in before. She had a new identity--Lana Loyalton. She stood and finger-combed her hair and knew she definitely was not the same person she had been. Sometimes she didn't recognize herself, how could someone else?

She checked the time and saw twenty minutes had gone by and Reno would be outside waiting. As she gathered her things scattered on the make-up counter, she glanced again at her watch.

It was the only thing, besides her mother's diamond and ruby earrings that she still had. A Timex, only a piece of junk, according to the environment Lindy moved in now, but it still held a lovely memory for her. The face was the size of a dime. The bracelet was a solid band of cheap gold. She slid it off her wrist and turned it over and read the inscription. Her eyes misted and the years peeled away as she remembered the bad times she had been going through then; haunting sleepless nights laced with doubts early on in her marriage. It had gone on for almost a year, then, abruptly stopped when they'd bought their house and become involved in renovating it. During that time her husband had given her the watch for a birthday present. The inscription on the inside read; Sweetheart, nightmares are only dreams! He had said it countless times to reassure her.

She ran her fingertip over the engraving, feeling the tiny edges of the letters on a faint ridge. A tiny sob welled up in her throat and she stood silently remembering the past. Then she lifted her head and gazed at herself in the mirror. A new woman stared back. Thinking clearly again after a few seconds of doubt, she straightened her shoulders, took a deep breath and dropped the watch in her purse. Slipping through the kitchen and a back exit, Lindy climbed into the white limousine and Reno sped her away.

***

John Thomas leaned on the bar at Tony's Steakhouse and nursed a whiskey. The raw liquor burned a path down his throat and matched the fire in his searing narcissistic revenge towards Reed Conners and Lindy Lewis.

He was pissed! Conners had disappeared and that meant Lindy Lewis was gone too! He'd dumped the black pick-up he'd stolen from that cowboy and now drove a plain car that he'd switched plates on. He'd bought clothes off a street thief and picked some pockets. He had guns and cash and knew he was cool. Hastily he made a phone call. After waiting a few minutes for his contact to check the computer, the man came back on the line. John Thomas sucked hard on his unfiltered cigarette as he listened to the man's whining voice as he said, "Okay, here's what I've got. First let me remind you Thomas, I expect my cut or I'll hunt you down!"

"You'll get it!" John Thomas fired back.

"Just so you don't forget!" The voice whined again.

"Right," John Thomas muttered into the receiver. Seconds later, he returned to the bar and gulped down the remainder of his whiskey, a swagger now in his step as he left intent on his mission. He was on his way to the Red Dog.

-32-

"What the hell happened Abby?" Reed asked, the telephone pressed to his ear. "I just talked to my boss and he said you were looking for me."

"Good Lord, I'm glad you called Reed. We didn't know where to find you!" Abby and her husband were his neighbors in the north who kept an eye on his place whenever he needed to leave.

Not telling her he'd been laid up after getting shot, he said, "I was out of commission for awhile. How bad is my place?"

"It's bad! Reed, the roof on your house buckled under the weight of the ice. That was last week. Joe and the boys covered the whole thing with plastic tarps."

"Shit," was all Reed could say.

"Listen, we're keeping an eye on the place, but when are you coming home?"   His neighbors,

Abby and Joe were old friends from way back. Retired and down to earth, they included Reed in their family of kids and grandkids. They were always concerned that he spent too much time alone.

"I shouldn't be too long. This case could be finished in a week or so." A grim look flashed over Reed's face as he answered.

"Oh Reed," Abby said catching her breath, "Everything is frozen in there!"

Reed's stomach lurched. "Does it look like anything can be salvaged ?"

"The windows are gone. And it looks like most of the damage is in the kitchen and living room," Abby said with a sigh. "We'd gone to visit some old friends in Chicago and got caught there. It lasted for days and ten inches of rain and snow fell. We lost the barn."

"Oh no, are you guys okay?"

"Oh, we're fine. Everyone has been helping each other out. Reed, you know that clump of birch by your back door? Well that's ruined too!"

"Oh shit," Reed muttered, "I heard something about storms up there. Freezing rain and below zero temperatures. It's been hotter than hell here."

"It's hard to imagine, we've been plowing snow and chopping ice for days," Abby said.

"Well, I guess the mess will have to stand until I get there. Can I give the insurance company your name to contact in the meantime?"

"That's fine Reed. We'll keep an eye on your place." After hanging up the phone, Reed sat down and ran his hands through his hair. He was sick at heart recalling all the months of backbreaking work he'd put into his home at the lake. Refinishing the oak cupboards and floors, putting in the three walls of windows that lined the kitchen and living room which looked out to the lake and the woods. The dining room table and chairs that he refinished the first winter had been in the family for generations. It was all a pile of frozen junk now. His breath caught. And his books! All the law books and his collections of Louie La'Mour, Mickey Spilane and John MacDonald!

He lit a cigarette and called the insurance company and was told he was just one of hundreds who had suffered damage from the storms and they'd get to him in a week or so. Christ, he had to finish this case and get home!

Manny had asked if he would recognize John Thomas, knowing Thomas was a master of deception, both in appearances and personality. Reed knew he would immediately recognize those evil eyes; no matter how he disguised himself.

When Thomas had been married to Reka Holmes, Tanner had described him as a partying tennis bum. Always dressed in Italian sweaters and Brooks Brothers clothes. Hair dyed and styled to perfection, thanks to Reka's money. When he'd masqueraded as Jud Thurman and infiltrated the insurance game, he'd worn conservative suits. Also a wig with short hair, mustache and glasses. He'd passed himself off as an out of town salesman and called himself J.T. when he'd romanced Lindy. But how would he disguise himself now?

Reed had purposely studied the faces of the regulars that hung out at the bar and was sure he could pick him out of the crowds that gyrated in and out of that pit of humanity at the Red Dog. As a lawyer, Reed had been good at reading people; picking up on the danger of closed emotions and sensing a sick mind. But, could he pick Thomas out in time, before Thomas singled him out? Reed's life depended on that!

Christ, he was tired of it all. The company was breathing down his neck to get the case wrapped up and now his home was smashed to hell. Reed slammed his fist down on the arm of the chair. Dust burst out and slowly sank down through the rays of sunshine that promised to heat up the day. A train rumbled by on near-by tracks just a block away, causing the floor and walls to shake. Reed got up and began to pace. He clenched a fist and slammed it into his other hand. The smacking noise echoed in the small room. Damn, he had to get out of there. He got in the Corvette. With hours to kill before the meeting with Manny and their stakeout at the Red Dog; he started to drive. Before long he was caught up in the fast paced traffic, shifting gears with his foot close to the floorboards. He drove aimlessly for several hours around downtown Dallas, over the huge traffic circles wherever the roads led. Now he understood the constant speed and the hustle of the city. He felt the emotions of the inhabitants; their need to hurry, get it done and get back. Exactly the way he felt at this moment. When he'd exhausted his impatience he made his way back to Flower Mound and stopped at Tony's Steakhouse, the same place Lindy had worked at. It was late in the afternoon and he needed some food and a drink. He slid up on a stool at the bar.

"Remember me?" Reed said after greeting the familiar bartender and laying out some cash.

"Sure Conners. You're usual?" As he busied himself pouring a whiskey for Reed, he turned and asked, "Did Betty tell you about this stranger asking about you a few days ago?"

"Yeah," Reed answered and looked around the bar; still in a foul mood. When his drink came he savored the tang of the whiskey on his tongue. Felt it slowly glide down his throat and its grip as it hit his stomach. He drew his cigarettes out of a pocket and flicked his lighter. As he raised his eyes over the bar after lighting up, they connected with a familiar face.

Son of a bitch, Reed muttered under his breath. He took another sip of his drink, placed his smoldering cigarette down in an ashtray and casually got off his stool. Without missing a beat, he walked around the bar and smashed his fist into the man's face and said, "Asshole, that's for what you did to Lindy Lewis!"

Dade Lampart lay on the floor, a surprised and pained look on his features as he tried to sit up, then mumbled, "Who the hell are you?"

Feeling a hundred percent better, Reed ignored him and the reaction of the surrounding patrons then calmly went back to his seat.

"Good job," the bartender said over the sudden rush of activity and winked at Reed as he wiped the counter.

"All in a day's work!" Reed downed his whiskey and left, unaware of the curious eyes that followed his exit.

-33-

Lindy walked with a determined step as she took her daily stroll on the beach. As she dressed that morning she had been shocked! There definitely was a sag in her body. A puckering had begun in her thighs and of all places, on her derrière.

How could this be happening? She was only forty-four years old! She was still young. How could the years be speeding by so fast, pushing her into middle age, when she still felt like a teenager? Well--, maybe not that young, but how unfair. She was just beginning her new life!

Unsettled by what she'd seen happening to her body, she called Mitzi when she got back to her condominium. "Hi," she said, "let's go to the Spa and spend the day."

"Oh Lindy," she gasped, "I can't afford that!"

"It's my treat." Lindy said as she stood draped in a towel after a shower. Her blonde hair hung in her eyes, the dark roots making a definite declaration.

"Really? That sounds wonderful Lindy. I need a lift."

Hearing the sobering edge in Mitzi's voice, Lindy asked her friend, "What's wrong?"

"I just heard from the authorities in Dallas. They've got Rocky in jail. This time he's going to be there for a long time."

Lindy huffed, "Well, do you really care? How can you after all the things he's done to you?"

"In a way I do feel bad. You know, things were good for us for awhile after he'd cleaned up his life."

"I know Mitzi, but he got involved in drugs again," Lindy reminded her.

"I know---, I'm just sorry about everything. We had a home and he was good to Mark." A few seconds went by as they both were silent.

"Mitzi, enough of the blues, let's spend the day getting beautiful. I'll pick you up." Hours later, they emerged from Saks Spa looking stunning and totally refreshed. They'd been wrapped, oiled, massaged, manicured and styled.

"Wow, you were right Lindy; this is exactly what I needed."

"See, I told you!" Lindy joked happily.

Reno helped them get settled in the limousine. "Where to ladies?" He asked and grinned at them in the rear view mirror as they sped out into traffic.

"I think we deserve a margarita, what do you think Mitzi?"

Mitzi smiled. "Sounds good, we look to good to go home!" As they drove away from the salon Lindy glanced out the back window of the limousine and her eyes widened in alarm as she recognized a car. It was the same black car that had followed her from the bank. The same man who had trailed her to the Diner was behind the wheel! A chill raced up her spine, but she pushed it away.

She'd been in Hilton Head for three weeks. Mario had been pursuing her, his attentions intriguing. Lindy hadn't succumbed to his charms, but he was wearing her down. They'd met for dinners and gone out on the yacht. She had a date with him that evening, alone, without Mitzi and Andre. Lindy had to admit she felt a tingle of excitement for this man; even though she told herself he was just a play-thing.

The girls found a table under an umbrella at a outside café and ordered margaritas. Lindy, smart in a lime green linen dress. Her painted nails glistened silver as she snapped a slim gold lighter and lit her cigarette. The holder clasped elegantly in the hand that showed off the new Rolex on her wrist. She felt wonderful.

"Lindy, have you decided to stay here in Hilton Head?" Mitzi asked minutes later as they sipped their frosty drinks.

"Yes, I think so," Lindy replied. "This is the kind of place I've always dreamed of." She swung her sandaled foot out from under the table and wiggled her toes, "Besides where would I go? How about you?"

"Well, I've got some potential jobs at the hospitals. If one comes through I've got to go back to Dallas to pick up our things." Mitzi looked happily at her friend.

"Really. Then what?" Lindy asked.

"Well, we can stay with my Mother for awhile and look for a place after I get settled into a job.

Cocktail hour had begun. The same combo of blond musicians that they'd seen before took the stage, this time playing soft romantic music. Suddenly, loneliness tugged at Lindy's heart as they played a familiar melody. It had been popular at the time her and her husband had been renovating the house. Anytime it came on they would drop whatever they were doing, grin at each other and sway to the strains of guitars.

"Oh God," she murmured to Mitzi, "that song still gets me right here." She placed a hand over her heart. Seeing the flicker of pain as it crossed Lindy's face, Mitzi reached out a comforting hand.

With a far away look in her eyes, Lindy looked out at the ocean and said, "I can't believe how things have changed. Here I am hundreds of miles from home, practically a fugitive on the run."

"Oh Lindy," Mitzi whispered, "don't think about it!"

Lindy sucked in her breath and said, "You're right. Let's have a refill."   The band changed tempos to an upbeat song and they soon tapped their toes to the music, both of them feeling better.

Lindy raised her glass. "Mitzi, I'm going out with Mario tonight. We're going out on the ocean and he promises a special night."

"I'm sure he does!" Mitzi eyed her friend. "What are you going to do if things heat up?"

"Well, I've thought about it. I'm not ready to get involved so I'll just string him along. Then again---." She smiled and smoothed her dress, checked her wonderful nails. They were long and tapered, thanks to the acrylics. But lord, she was always stabbing herself, and had a bitch of a time getting dressed. Just then two girls walked by going out to the beach wearing bikinis, their chests overflowing their skimpy tops. Lindy and Mitzi started to giggle. Oh brother, they whispered. But, Lindy couldn't get an idea out of her head. Something she'd thought about for years and especially since seeing the drastic change in her body.

"You know Mitzi," she confided, "I've been thinking I just might get that done and more!"

"What?" Mitzi's glass clunked down on the plastic topped table. Lindy leaned in closer and whispered, "boobs!" She put her hands out in front of her chest to emphasize dimensions.

"Good lord," Mitzi exclaimed, "You must be drunk! Do you know how painful that is?"

"Well no--," Lindy whispered, "but, I'm tired of the miracle bra, and everything is starting to pucker and sag!"

"Lindy, you can't be serious! You look just fine. Give me another of those smokes." They finished their drinks, and Lindy stood up.

"I've got to run; Mario is picking me up at eight o'clock. But, I'll call you tomorrow and let you know how the night went."

****

"Mama, mia," Mario exclaimed as he stood at Lindy's door. His eyes swept over her appreciatively, "Be still my heart," he added.

After she got home, Lindy showered, refreshed her make-up and dressed in a slinky black dress. The hemline ended above her knees and her feet were in high-heeled black sandals. Her newly lightened blonde hair swept back off her face to show off her mother's diamond and ruby earrings glistening on her ears.

She smiled at his charming words, looked him over with approval and thought he looked like someone from a cover of GQ. Dressed in a light colored taupe suit, the jacket casually opened over a black silk tee shirt, with black loafers on his bare feet. Brown eyes and dark curly hair accentuated the golden tan of his Italian features with a few lines springing out at the corners of his eyes when he smiled.

They walked hand in hand down the boardwalk to the marina and stepped onto the yacht as lights began to blink on back on the shore. As they sat and relaxed in chaise lounges, the craft manned by an unseen navigator began to move out on the ocean. The lights became smaller in the distance, the night cool. A bottle of champagne lay chilled in a silver bucket and soft music encased them in an intimate circle as Pavarotti crooned a love song.

The motion of the yacht lulled Lindy into a melancholy mood as bubbles burst from the wine and tickled her nose. Along with the margaritas she'd drank earlier with Mitzi, she felt marvelous.

Abruptly, Mario stood up and swept her into his arms and as she fit herself into his embrace, her sudden need matched his fire.

-34-

As Reed drove away from Tony's Steakhouse he flexed his wrist. Goddamn, it had hurt like hell when his knuckles connected with Dade Lampart's jaw, but the gratification was worth it! Maybe he'd go back and finish the sucker off later. Oh hell, Reed grumbled to himself, the guy is a loser and not worth wasting time on, but he did make a call. "Here's a tip for you," he said to the Dallas authorities, "Check the Silver Dollar spread, highway 101, ten miles out. The place is overrun with illegals." Now he felt better yet!

Traffic was horrendous on the Dallas freeways. The speed limit said seventy, but everyone was going eighty or eighty-five miles an hour. The Corvette sailed expertly with the rest of the natives. Reed's stomach growled, knotted up with hunger pangs. His nerves strung to the limit. A sheen of sweat glistened on his face even though the air-conditioner hummed smoothly as he neared the Red Dog. As he slowed to find a parking spot, he slipped his dark aviator glasses on and a cap low on his head. Then he opened the glove compartment and slid the .38 in his waistband under his shirt.

"Jesus Ruby, you still haven't gotten the air fixed in this hell-hole," he muttered as he leaned on the bar. Ruby puckered up her lips and blew him a kiss.

"Hello to you too." She placed two beers down in front of him on the bar. The extra one for Manny, as usual. Reed's body was tense. His eyes hard behind the dark lenses as he scanned the crowd. Hank William Junior's voice competed with the raucous of the late day revelers. Reed took a drink of the dark strong beer. It burned his throat, but fed his hunger.

Manny appeared at his side. His voice barely audible above the noise as he muttered, "Buddy." Reed nodded for him to follow to their usual place at the end of the bar. Directly across from the door.

"Anything new?" Manny asked after tilting his bottle and taking a gulping swallow. He wiped his mustache on the back of his hand as his eyes searched Reed's face.

"Nope!" They leaned in close to each other as they talked, elbows pressed against the guns under their shirts. Their eyes moved cautiously over the crowd.

The bar was dark. Candles stuck in wine bottles perched on the scarred tables that covered the middle of the room. High backed booths lined three sides of the place and a dance floor took up space on the rough wood floors, encrusted with dirt and years of spills. The slap of pool table balls echoed from across the room. Whiskey, sweat, grease and smoke contributed to the ambience. Liquor signs were plastered on the walls and over the bar a huge picture of inviting red lips.

Reed blew out a cloud of smoke from his cigarette and said, "I just heard from up north, and goddamn, the roof on my house collapsed from ice built up from a storm!"

"A storm?" Manny asked.

"Yeah, smashed to hell!" Reed let out a disgusted grunt.

"You mean a tornado?"

"Christ no, an ice storm!"

Manny looked at him and said, "It's still summer man."

Just then Reed stiffened, jabbed Manny in the ribs. "That's him!" he whispered. He set the beer bottle down and air hissed in his throat as he inhaled. They watched as John Thomas swaggered to the bar. Dressed in faded jeans and a black tee-shirt, a Western straw hat pulled down over his eyes did not hide his identity from Reed. The air in the room dripped with humidity as they watched Thomas order a drink and throw some bills on the bar.

"Now," Reed barked in Manny's ear. They made their way through the crowd, each of them taking a different route. The hair on Reed's neck stiff as it caught on his shirt collar as he moved. Manny stopped and ran his hand over a waitress's hip, whispered in her ear and watched Reed's progress through the maze of people out of the corner of his eye. Just as Thomas raised the drink glass to his lips, both men stood at his side, guns jammed in his back.

"Move and your dead!" Reed growled.

Thomas froze. The glass dropped out of his hand, crashed and splattered to the floor. No one noticed. Just another drunk. In an instant they had his arms pinned.

Thomas turned to Reed and snarled, "Fuck you Conners," his foul breath hit Reed in the face.

"Nice and slow," Reed said as they shoved him to the door. The crowd parted, unconcerned. Once outside, Manny slipped the handcuffs on Thomas' wrist and called the station. All the while Reed had the .38 held at his head.

"I've got Lindy!" Thomas jeered.

"Yeah?" The gun in Reed's hand increased its pressure to Thomas's head.

"Ha, she came crawling, begged me to take her back." Thomas stood arrogantly, his eyes flat. He lurched towards Reed. The .38 jerked.

"Save it asshole." Reed's breath came out in a huff.

"She's not too bad in bed," Thomas went on.

Reed jammed the gun harder to his head.

"Sex, money, all waiting for me." Thomas rocked back on his heels and smirked. "Hate to tell you this Conners, but, she'll do anything I want her to. Just took a little persuasion." He spit in Reed's face.

Metal cracked on bone and Thomas fell to the ground. As he lay sprawled in the dirt, blood sprang from his nose. Reed shoved the gun in his waistband, picked Thomas up by the shirt-front and punched him. Then dropped him.

"Motherfucker," Thomas mumbled spewing blood.

Reed growled, "Say it again, asshole."

"Fuck you."

"You just don't learn, do you?" All reason had left Reed's senses as he picked Thomas up again and punched him in the stomach, then let him fall to the ground.

"Easy buddy." Manny said and pushed Reed aside.

Thomas lay still, then said "Motherfucker," again out of swollen lips. Reed's cap and glasses had fallen off, his sweat soaked sandy hair fell over his forehead. His face, red and mottled with anger. His breath cracked as he moved around Manny and grabbed Thomas, standing him up again. This time, his knee connected with his groin. Thomas doubled over, cried out in pain and passed out.

"Christ, I think you killed him," Manny mumbled.

"Nah, he's too mean to die," Reed said as he picked up his cap and wiped the dirt off his glasses. Sirens screamed as patrol cars screeched to a stop. They loaded Thomas in and drove off, but not before they asked why he was so bloody.

"He fell!" Reed said.

"Reed, what are you going to do now?" Manny asked several hours later as they sat in his office and finished paperwork, then sent it on to the chief.

Pissed, Reed shook his head. After all this time he was back to where he had started. Thomas in jail, and Lindy Lewis still missing!

"I've got to get back up north to take care of things. Then--, I'll see." He exhaled and stuck out his hand and said, "Thanks buddy for all your help, I'll keep you posted!" He went back to his room and packed. But there was something he had to do before leaving. On a hunch, he picked up the phone.

-35-

On the yacht Amour as Lindy and Mario kissed, the heat of their passion melded them together in a long embrace. Mario groaned and slid his hands down her back, clasping her hips to him. He murmured in her ear as he plied her with hot licks; on her neck, her shoulders, then pushed aside the shoulder strap on her dress and found a nipple. His arms, strong and binding. Lindy's body throbbed and all her resolutions disappeared in the breeze.

Groaning, Mario picked her up and carried her into the bedroom. He laid her down on the bed as their tongues explored the depths of their sensations. Lindy held her breath as he moved down her chest, nibbled again on her nipples, caressed her stomach and her thighs. Her breath exploded then as he found her mound of womanhood and exquisitely brought her to completion. She lay relaxed as he moved to slip her dress off. When she sat up to slip her shoes off, he murmured "No, leave them on."

Mario caressed her lovingly, his breath heavy as his mouth closed on hers again. Lindy's ears roared, her thoughts spun. Just then a knock echoed on the door of the bedroom suite. Mario's body stiffened as the sound vibrated again, this time louder. He cursed in Italian and stood up, adjusted his clothes and went to the door. After a few whispered words, he stepped out and closed the door. Lindy pulled a cover over herself, lost in the erotic sensations Mario had brought out in her.

She was suddenly jerked fully awake as the yacht began to rock. She laid still, her body tensed as she listened. The roar of another motor came nearer and nearer. Curiously, she stood up, wrapped herself in a sheet and stumbled to a small window in the dark room. She parted the drapes and peeked out. Her eyes widened in alarm, as another large ship quietly slid to their side. Lindy moved to the side of the window and caught a glimpse of Mario looking on. The motors of both ships at a low hum now. A man stepped onto the Amour and joined Mario. Just then a beam of moonlight caught the face of the other man. Lindy gasped, then clamped a hand over her mouth. It was Jason Agar! The man who had followed her from the bank and the Diner. Her knees buckled and she clung to the window frame for support.

She watched as the two men exchanged packages. Then as Agar opened his container, reached in and put a finger to his lips, Mario ripped open a box. Their voices grew loud. Horrified, Lindy watched as Mario pointed a gun at Agar and Agar fell backwards. Then Mario bent over and retrieved the package, pushing him over the side of the boat and into the water. Mario stood for a moment and then to her horror, she thought he glanced right at the window where she stood. Lindy grabbed the wall to steady herself then fell to the floor as the ship suddenly jerked into motion. She sat clutching the sheet around herself as her heart burst into a wild beat.

Good Lord, Mario had killed the man. He was a murderer! Her breath caught, as she realized she was trapped with a killer out in the middle of the ocean. She was a prisoner on the boat. She scrambled back to the bed, her eyes wild as she searched the room for something. Something she could use for protection. In the moonlight her gaze landed on a heavy fluted crystal vase on the bedside table, matching a nearby ashtray. She moved it closer. All she needed was a plan.

A minute went by, then five, ten. She tried to still her pounding heart, then stretched out on the bed. The sheet covered her breasts and thighs. Her feet still in her high heeled shoes. She took long deep breaths and willed her nerves to quiet. Just then she heard the door open and felt Mario's presence as he moved into the room. A chill spread up her back. She heard a thud as he dropped something on the floor. In an instantaneous reflex, she raised an arm to protect herself.

"Lindy," he murmured and lay down on the bed and began kissing her again.

My God, he'd just shot a man and tossed him in the ocean, and now wanted to resume their love-making! Lindy's mind worked furiously. She had to get out of there, somehow! Her hands went over his back and up to his shoulders.

"You're so tense Mario," she murmured in a husky voice, "Turn over and I'll relax you. It'll make our love better." Mario moved his shoulders up and down and groaned. Lindy guided him onto his stomach and then slid on his back and began to massage. Murmuring softly.

"There my love," she crooned, "let my fingers take away the aches and tensions. Feel the magic." Her heart lurched and she held her breath, picked up the vase and brought it down on his head. Her face paled at the thudding sound. She stared at his still body.

Oh God, had she killed him? She fumbled on the floor, picked up her dress, slipped it on and patted her hair. She bent over him and listened to his chest. Finally she heard a faint breath.

The ship bobbed furiously as they sped over the ocean waves. She stood hanging on to the foot of the bed to keep her balance. He was alive, but when he came to, he'd know she'd seen the drugs and the murder! She'd tie him up. That's what they did in movies. She looked around the room for something, and then stumbled over to a closet. She flung the door open and found a suit of clothes; complete with tie, belt, and handkerchief. Her hands shook as she grabbed it off a hanger and went back over to the bed. She rolled Mario over, not looking at his handsome pale face and his closed eyes. A trail of saliva clung to his chin.

She had to hurry, if he awakened now--. Perspiration streaked her face, smudged her mascara and mingled with her perfume as she struggled to tie his hands behind his back with the necktie. Then she wound the belt around his ankles and stuffed the hanky in his mouth. Done! She ran to the door and glanced back. Oh no! He might be able to roll out of the room somehow. She grabbed the tie that stretched around his wrists and wound it around the bedpost. Now, he couldn't go anywhere!

As Lindy ran to the bedroom door and opened it her foot kicked against something and she picked up Mario's gun. She'd need that, she thought. She saw lights twinkling in the distance and she watched now her heart caught in her throat.

Were they going back to Hilton Head or headed to some strange port? She shivered in the damp night air as the ship's motor hummed and finally neared the shore. Suddenly, as they rounded a bend, a red and white lighthouse appeared and she recognized Harbor Town. They were back to where they'd started from. The ship slowed as they neared the marina and the boardwalk came into view. Before the anchor hit the water, Lindy took off running with the gun hidden under her arm.

She'd gotten away!   As she tried to still her trembling body, she looked back at the yacht and saw everything was quiet. Whoever was manning the craft apparently was busy tying it down. She tossed the gun into the marsh, smoothed her hair as she sucked in air and struggled to still the shakes as she hurried to her condo. Thank God, it wasn't more than a couple of blocks. Reaching the safety of the building, she stopped at the desk and asked the clerk to open her door.

"My evening bag was stolen!" she said faintly.

"No problem, Miss Loyalton," the man replied as he followed her to her rooms. After he left she locked the door and collapsed.

But, how soon would it be before someone came after her? She had to leave. She had to get away, now! She began to throw her clothes on the bed. All her beautiful things landed in a heap. Her make-up rattled on the vanity in the bathroom as she loaded them into a case. Within ten minutes she was packed and flying down the back stairs to the garage for her car. The powerful BMW roared to life as she flew out onto the drive. She glanced at her watch. The Rolex gleamed in the dash lights and pointed to ten o'clock PM. Hard to believe, only a few hours had gone by since she'd walked down to the marina with Mario with stars in her eyes.

She drove, speeding to the end of the island and then over the bridge that divided South Carolina proper from the island. The night was dark as velvet. The air heavy with the smell of the swamp that lined the highway on both sides. Tall trees grew out of the water, laden with gray moss that swung in the breeze, casting shadow-like arms that reached threateningly towards Lindy's car as she sped by.

What would she do now? Where could she go? All her money was back in the Plaza Bank in Hilton Head.

Oh God, she needed to think! She drove aimlessly for hours and finally settled for a motel room to rest and figure out what to do.

Laurie Lawson, she'd written on the registration. The sun was up, the birds happily chattering away at the new day as Lindy fell into bed. After several hours of sleep she drove back to Hilton Head and circled the bank twice before she dared park and go in.

Would the police be there waiting for her and arrest her for killing Mario? So far so good, but her hand shook as she put the key in her safe deposit box. Maybe Mario would be there somewhere and grab her on the way out! With an idea in mind she walked up to a security guard and asked, "Would you walk me to my car please? I'm feeling faint all of a sudden."

Concerned, the man looked at her and said, "Sure Miss. But do you want me to call 911?"

"Oh no thanks, it's just a bug I picked up. I'll be fine as soon as I get home." He smiled at her and took her arm. Minutes later, Lindy was on the road again. Her money tucked safely under the car seat. As the sun streamed over the lonely South Carolina swamps, tears slid down her face.

Why had everything gone wrong again? Now she had to leave Hilton Head and get away fast. Far away from Mario! There was only one person

who could help her. But, would he? She drove on
in the black BMW heading north.

-36-

The days and nights were a blur to Lindy as she drove through the southern states, stopping only to catch a few hours of sleep and a quick meal. Fear tugged at her heels as she kept an eye on the rearview mirror. Her hands shook on the steering wheel when a car seemed to get too close, followed too long, or when she saw a face that resembled Mario. As the miles began to separate her from the sunny south and bring her closer to her roots, she sighed with loneliness. She had no one who really cared, except Reed Conners and maybe it was too late.

In Iowa light snow began as she traveled through the windswept countryside. Here, the stripped corn fields stood in forlorn lines of frozen stalks and the woods were bleak and bare. As Lindy listened to the radio the music stopped and an announcer said, "Folks, don't forget to buy your turkey, its count-down time until the big day." Tears started as a familiar surge of pain crawled through her heart as she remembered all those happy Thanksgiving gatherings with her husband, family and friends.

The prairie winds whistled as she drove on huddled in the darkness. As she neared Minneapolis, wet snow began to stick to the car windows and limited her visibility. At a familiar crossing, curiosity led her to the old neighborhood and she turned off the freeway and followed a country road. Over time the open fields had filled with homes. It was so different from the time when they'd first moved there. Lindy slowed to a stop.

She hadn't been back since she stood outside in the March wind and watched her house burn, clutching her old red robe. Her breath caught as she stared out the car window at the place where her home had been. The ground was flat and bare. All her lilac bushes and maple trees were gone. The long curved driveway that her husband had labored on for weeks, buckled with dead weeds growing out of the crevices, frozen now in the drifts of ice and snow. The only reminder that anything had ever stood there was the chimney, standing alone and awkwardly reaching upward. A sob wrenched through her thoughts. Things had been so good then. No worries. Just the blind assumption that her happiness would go on and on.

Had she known that she would end up alone in that house, battling endless repairs and loneliness, she never would have insisted they buy that mausoleum and work their fingers to the bone restoring it. It had been beautiful though. Lindy sighed and wiped her eyes. They had finally finished and settled into enjoying the splendor of their efforts.

Lord, she also remembered her bewilderment at seeing those cracks begin to appear in the ceilings; the walls and the foundation. Then there came the confirmation that carpenter ants had taken over her home. Burning it to the ground was the only thing she could have done, she concluded for the umpteenth time. And she had started a new life with the insurance money. She had been rich and carefree.

But what had gone wrong? The money had not brought her the happiness she thought she could find. Only danger from J.T., Dade Lampart and now Mario. She shivered as she remembered seeing Mario kill. Would Reed help her now? And going back meant she'd really have to return the money. That was a sobering thought!

She shifted the car into drive and left her old neighborhood. Well, she'd give it back and start over! If she drove all night, she could be at Reed's by morning. She stopped at a convenience store for coffee. As Lindy started the last leg of her journey, snow and ice began to cover the highway. The radio said a blizzard was in store. She blew on the hot coffee, taking small sips as the night continued in a dark lonely vacuum.

Finally, as the sun began to send streaks of pink and violet over the sky, the countryside appeared, covered in a white blanket. Lindy opened the window and inhaled the cold crisp air to clear her head. The wind tousled her blond hair. She was on the last few miles of the familiar gravel road that wound through the woods and curved around the lake.

There it was. The birch trees were bare. Pines, tall and stately as she remembered. Reed's home! She bravely drove up the driveway and then sat, aghast at what she saw.

There were no comforting lights glowing through the windows. No wisp of smoke trailing upward from the chimney. Nothing but a broken shell of the house covered in blue plastic tarps, heaped with ice and snow.

Lindy had a terrifying thought. Had Mario done this? Had he shot Reed too? She huddled in the car as frantic thoughts ran through her head. After seeing him kill that man on his yacht, she knew he'd kill again and now she was sure she would be next! She took a shaking breath as she sat paralyzed with fear. And he would steal her money too.

No way is that murderer going to get my fortune! She peered through the frosty car windows and pondered. Suddenly she remembered just the right place to hide it. What better place than on Reed's property? She thought slyly and reached for the shoe-box from under the seat and got out of the car. She dashed across the yard and past the dock where J.T. had her cornered. Through the grove of trees to an abandoned shack that stood forgotten and out of sight from the house. Her shoes sliding on the frozen ground. She pulled the creaking door open and peered in. Cobwebs hung from the ceiling. Leaves and rusty junk lay scattered just as she remembered it when her and Reed had gone exploring his acreage so many years ago. Her gaze fell on an old tin pail. Just the thing she needed. She fit the shoe-box in it and covered it with boards. There. Her money was safe!

Lindy ran back to her car, but just as she was ready to leave a Corvette roared into the driveway. She sucked in her breath as Reed got out of his car and stared at his house for long minutes, then turned his burning gaze at her. He glared at her as she opened the car door and stepped out.

"Where the hell have you been? I've been all over the country looking for you," he yelled.

In her sagging sweats, with dark circles under her eyes, Lindy's voice trembled. "I came back," was all she could manage.

"Goddamn, do you have any idea what you've put me through?" His voice was cold. "Goddamn it Lindy, give me those car keys and get in my car. We're going into town!"

Now she was really frightened. He must be taking her to the police station!

"Please Reed," she begged as she handed him the keys to her BMW. Then turned her tear filled eyes to him and whispered brokenly, "I need to talk to you. Please Reed? I need your help!"

"Jesus Christ, what is it now?" He pushed his sandy hair off his forehead and continued, "This better be good. I'm warning you for the last time Lindy, this is it!" He glared at her again.

As she clamored into his car, had she seen just a little bit of concern in his eyes? "What happened to your house?" she asked then to change the subject.

"Christ, a storm loaded the roof with ice. Goddamn, if I'd been here instead of wasting time trying to find you, it wouldn't have happened!" Lindy cringed as he gunned the motor in his car and they headed into town. He drove up to the one and only motel.

"I need a place to stay," he grumbled. He tossed the key on a table after they entered the small rooms. "Now Lindy," he said warily, "start at the beginning, but I'll remind you, you're charged with arson, with intent to defraud the insurance company!"   Lindy sank into an easy chair and shivered. Her face paled as he continued, "And now they have your taking off to add to the charges! What the hell are you doing?"

Well, here it was. There was no way out. She had to come clean and tell Reed everything so he would help her, or sooner or later Mario would find her.

She took a deep shaking breath and began. Reed listened with his face grim. When she got to the part about how she had been on the yacht and watched Mario murder Jason Agar, he sat up. His voice cracked as he fired questions at her. Finally, she had confessed everything to him. Then he asked the dreaded question.

"Where is the money Lindy?"

Lindy's face was mottled with tears. A tissue lay torn to shreds in her hands and without hesitating she said, "In a safe deposit box in Hilton Head, South Carolina." Well, she had told him just about everything. That had just slipped out!

"I've got some calls to make," Reed said going to the phone. She tried to read his thoughts as he continued, "You may as well get some rest while you can," and nodded towards the bedroom. She went into the room and huddled under the covers.

Sometime later Reed came into the room and said, "We've got an appointment with a judge in thirty minutes. Maybe you might want to change clothes and fix up some."

Lindy stood up, her legs weak. "What's going to happen," she asked faintly?

"That's what we're going to find out!" Reed turned away and went back to the paperwork he had spread on a table. By the look on his face, Lindy guessed it was all over for her. It meant prison!

The afternoon was a blur to her. Papers were exchanged between hands. Faces darted into focus and faded. Finally through the fog in her head Lindy heard Reed say, "Your honor, I'm going to pay the fifty thousand dollar fine!"

"You do understand Mr. Conners," the judge said," that you will be responsible for Miss Lewis. Since she has helped solve that case in the south and I'm being extremely lenient here, I'm dropping the charges. But she has to make restitution in three days. That means every last cent has got to be repaid to the insurance company. One million dollars!"

"Yes your honor. Thank you," Reed said as the gavel echoed and chairs scraped on the wood floor and the unknown faces left the room. Lindy sat dumbstruck, unable to move. Reed took her arm and propelled her out of the courthouse and into his car.

"Reed, does this mean, I won't have to go to jail?" she whispered.

"Lindy, you're damn lucky the judge is a fishing buddy! We were able to make a deal in exchange for information about the murder scene in South Carolina. You were traveling in some dangerous company!" Lindy's hands trembled in her lap.

Reed started the Corvette and gunned the motor as he said, "Mario D'Agustino and his brother are international drug dealers. Mario killed Jason Agar who was an FBI agent. The FBI had lost their trail until you pin-pointed their whereabouts."

"Oh my God!" This was worse than she thought. She sagged against the back of the car seat.

"We'll fly down to Hilton Head and pick up the money in the morning," Reed said then and Lindy froze. Oh God, she had to tell him they didn't have to go. That the money was right there hidden in his shack! Well maybe, she'd wait awhile until he seemed calmer.

The sun set as they walked across the street to the local café for dinner where Lindy ordered a brandy Manhattan to relieve her stress. Then another one for courage. When their meal came she decided to tell him when they got back to the motel. When they got there she was totally relaxed and didn't want to break the spell, but asked curiously, "Reed, where'd you get all that money?"

Reed had slipped off his jacket, hung it in the closet and turned to her. "I picked up a check from my insurance company today to cover the expenses to rebuild my house." He sat down in an easy chair.

"You mean you would use that for me?"

"Was I wrong going out on a limb for you?" His eyes held hers.

Lindy stood up and went over to him. "Reed, I don't know what to say." She leaned down and kissed him. "I'll work and pay you back. Every cent," she declared tearfully.

"Are you through running now?" With good intentions, Lindy nodded her head, wiped her eyes and slipped into his arms. Reed's embrace tightened around her and as their kisses deepened he groaned and led her to the bed. They made love, hot and passionate, then sweet and gentle. Lindy lay content, happy at last in Reed's arms.

When she awoke the next morning she found a note propped up on the bedside table from him that read, "I'm getting coffee from the café, be back shortly. Our flight leaves for Hilton Head this afternoon."

Oh God, she had completely forgotten again to tell him that they didn't need to go! She reread the note and climbed back into bed. As soon as he gets back I'll tell him, she thought. He'd be mad; but maybe not too mad. After all they'd just made love!

Seeing it was still early she pulled the covers around herself. Dozing off she fell into a dream. She was standing in a kitchen. Reed's kitchen. She could tell by the row of windows that opened out over the lake. She was scraping dishes for the dishwasher. A sandy-hair toddler had a hold of her ankle. A rosy-cheeked, two year old sat in a highchair and with a practiced hand threw her applesauce. It splattered and covered the cupboards then dripped to the floor.

Recognizing herself as the woman in the dream she cringed as she heard herself yell, "Reed Conners, I need some help." Too late, she realized he was out of town again on a case. She wiped her tired eyes on a sleeve, got down and wiped up the floor.

Oh God, the work, the kids and endless laundry. She groaned in her sleep and then awoke with the dream ingrained in her mind.

Was this what was in store for her? It wasn't a dream, it was a nightmare! She tossed and turned in Reed's bed as she weighed the possible future.

"I can't do it," she whispered to the silence in the motel room in the small peaceful town. I'm sorry Reed, I'm just not ready! She hesitated for a minute just to make sure and then hugged his pillow for the last time.

She threw on some clothes and grabbed Reed's car keys that lay on a table. Then raced out of the motel parking lot and down to his house at the lake where her beautiful black BMW stood just where she'd left it, and she had an extra key!

Lindy's anxious breath burned her throat as she ran through the brush and weeds to the shack and uncovered the shoebox filled with her million dollars. She forced her hands to be still as she painstakingly counted out fifty thousand dollars to repay Reed and placed the money in his car.

And within minutes as the freeway beckoned Lindy Lewis, his town faded into the background.

The End

TO ORDER COPIES OF THIS BOOK

SEND $12.99 TO

KIELEY PUBLISHING
P. O. Box 58 ST.MICHAEL, MN 55376
OR GO TO gennykieleybooks.com

While you're there check out these other Novels from
KIELEY PUBLISHING
and NIGHT WRITERS.

NIGHTMARES
AND DREAMS

LYN MILLER
LACOURSIER

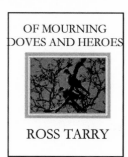

OF MOURNING
DOVES AND HEROES

ROSS TARRY

Nightmares and Dreams
By Lyn Miller LaCoursiere
300 Pages............$12.99

Of Mourning Doves
and Heroes
By Ross Tarry
208 Pages.....$12.99

Coming Soon
Cardinal Red, Last Cry of the Whipporwill,
Sunsets, Tomorrow's Rain, and Suddenly Summer.

**Make sure to include your name, address
with city, state & zip code.
Add $2.50 for postage on each book.**